The Mystery of the White Knuckle Ride

Alex gripped the sides of his seat. Was the ride going too fast? Could it come off its tracks and hurl them all into space? For the first time he was scared, and looking round he saw the others were as petrified as he was. Ben, wild-eyed and frozen, sat next to Emily who was screaming but not with excitement. Next to him, Kate seemed transfixed, droplets of sweat starting out on her forehead.

'Stop,' yelled the woman behind them. 'Stop!' But the ride went even faster, roaring down the descents and pulling up the slopes with incredible force.

First published in Great Britain in 1996
by Macdonald Young Books
61 Western Road
Hove
East Sussex
BN3 1JD

Photoset in North Wales by
Derek Doyle & Associates, Mold, Clwyd.
Printed and bound in Great Britain by
The Guernsey Press Co. Ltd.

British Library Cataloguing in Publication Data available.

ISBN: 0 7500 2161 6
ISBN: 0 7500 2162 4 (pb)

The Marlow House

MYSTERIES

3

THE MYSTERY OF THE WHITE KNUCKLE RIDE

•

Anthony Masters

MACDONALD YOUNG BOOKS

THE MARLOW HOUSE MYSTERIES

1

The Mystery of Bloodhound Island

2

The Mystery of the Shadow Caves

3

The Mystery of the White Knuckle Ride

4

The Mystery of Captain Keene's Treasure

· 1 ·

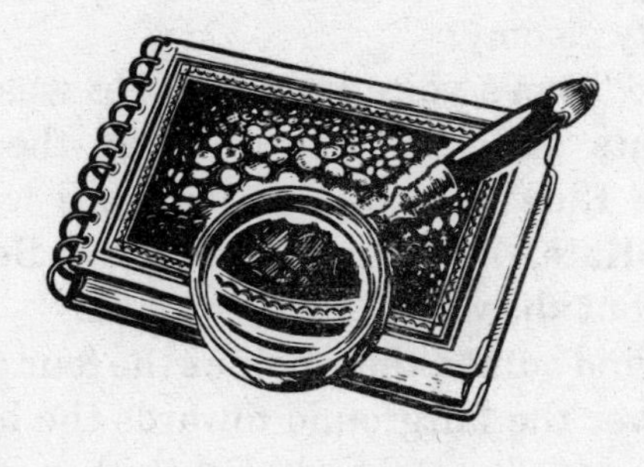

'We've stopped,' said Ben nervously.

'We're meant to stop,' said Alex. 'It's a frightener.'

Emily shivered. 'It's also a long drop.'

'Well, this *is* the White Knuckle Ride,' pointed out Kate. 'What do you expect?'

They had all expected to scream their heads off, for the ride was new and the pride of Sam Shepherd's Fairground. The place had only been open a few months, and for a first season had done good business, but that wasn't surprising. Tremaron's only other attraction was the Roxy Amusement Arcade, which was small and cramped and in need of a lick of paint.

Still the ride didn't start.

'I don't get it,' said Kate.

'I've got this feeling we're stuck.' Emily was decidedly gloomy.

'Stuck?' Ben's voice trembled. He was afraid of heights and had only come on the White Knuckle Ride so as not to lose face with the others. Kate, his sister, knew how Ben was feeling, but she wasn't going to let on.

The wind ruffled their hair as the four of them gazed over the fairground towards the harbour and the sea. It was early September and the tourist season was almost finished.

'Stuck?' Ben repeated, looking down at the insect-like crowd below. He felt a swaying, drawing sensation as if the iron safety bar was about to spring open and plunge him down to the distant ground.

'It's all right,' said Kate. 'We're bound to start moving soon.'

'If we don't,' replied Ben shakily, 'something's going to start moving inside me.'

'You can't throw up here,' protested Alex.

'Why not?' Ben tried hard not to look down,

but the more he tried, the more he looked.

The fairground wasn't large. Apart from a few stalls and a coconut shy, there was a Hall of Mirrors, a Ghost Maze and a roundabout with beautifully painted wooden horses. He could see the old woman who ran the hoopla stall cycling away on what looked like a brand new bike. Its polished chrome winked up at him, catching the sun.

Sam Shepherd, the owner of the fair, had once been a fisherman but had later made money selling secondhand cars. He was Alex's uncle, a big, burly man with a luxuriant moustache. He had always wanted to be a showman and now his ambition was fulfilled, although the fairground had to keep paying its way and the season was limited. What was more, Bill Buxton owned a much larger site at Penlyn, a small town a mile up the coast, and they were already locked in fierce competition.

'But isn't anyone going to *do* anything?' complained Ben, whose face was now grey and drawn.

'We'll get going in a minute,' said Emily soothingly. 'Don't worry.'

'That's what everyone keeps saying, but we've been stuck here for hours.'

'Minutes,' corrected Kate.

'It *feels* like hours,' he grumbled.

Alex gazed down to see if he could catch sight of his uncle, but there was no sign of him. Alex was Kate and Ben's closest friend since their parents had moved from London to run the Marlow House hotel on the quayside.

'Don't you think we ought to try and attract someone's attention?' asked Emily who, like Alex, came from the local fishing community.

'I would have thought it was pretty obvious something was wrong,' observed Kate. 'We're all meant to be screaming our heads off, not sitting up here like idiots.'

'I *will* be screaming my head off in a minute,' said Ben with feeling.

'Do you get vertigo?' asked Emily, getting the message at last.

'The fear of heights,' muttered Alex. 'You never told us.'

'I'm OK if I'm doing something or I'm not up for long,' explained Ben unhappily. 'This is long.'

'That's right,' said a woman in another car a little further back. 'It shouldn't be allowed.'

'Disgraceful,' added her husband.

'I want to get down,' sobbed a young child. 'I want to get down *now*.'

'Where's Uncle Sam?' demanded Alex. 'Surely

he can't be in the pub?' He looked at his watch anxiously. It was just after four on a Saturday afternoon.

'You management, are you?' shouted the husband.

'Mr Shepherd's my uncle,' replied Alex. 'He can't help what's happened here,' he added defensively.

'He ought to make sure this ride's safe,' said the wife.

'It *is* safe.' Alex was getting angry now. 'We're *all* safe.'

'Then what are we doing stuck up here?'

'I think I can see Cliff. He's one of my uncle's engineers. He'll soon fix it.'

'He'd better,' observed the woman ominously.

'What's he going to do, Alex?' gasped Ben miserably, gazing down again compulsively.

Cliff Baker had a megaphone in his hand. He was a tall, good-looking nineteen-year-old with long, glossy black hair and a cheeky, challenging smile. Like Alex and Emily, he had been born and bred in Tremaron, and after leaving school had worked in the local garage until Sam had hired him.

'Don't worry,' Cliff said through the megaphone, his voice reassuring. 'I'll soon have you down.'

'How?' shouted the woman. 'You going to fetch a ladder?'

'A ladder?' Ben's stomach lurched. 'I'm not going down on a ladder.'

'I'm going to crank you down,' Cliff yelled into the megaphone.

'Sounds painful,' said Emily, a flicker of amusement in her green eyes. She glanced across at Alex and he winked at her. They'd become great friends and both loved Tremaron. Neither could imagine life away from the little Cornish fishing town, with its steep winding streets and busy, working quayside.

Alex was stockily built and cautious. He loved the sea and couldn't wait to join his father and brothers on the trawlers when he left school. Emily was much more impetuous and was often guided by instinct. Even now she was quite sure they were going to be safe.

Ben wasn't usually scared; he just had a bad feeling for heights. Normally he was very positive, and because he was tall for his age he often appeared to be taking the lead. His sister, Kate, on the other hand, was as impulsive as Emily and didn't always bother to think things through. Kate was eleven, a year younger than the others, but saw to it that they treated her as an equal.

None of them had been on the White Knuckle Ride before. Usually they spent most of their time sailing together; despite the fact that Sam Shepherd was Alex's uncle they had taken little interest in the new fairground. Now, just before they went back to school, they had decided to give the White Knuckle a try.

Suddenly, without the slightest warning, the White Knuckle Ride jerked into life and began to clank down the incline at an increasing pace.

'No,' shouted Ben. 'This can't be happening.'

In a blur, Kate caught sight of Cliff dropping his megaphone and running towards the control room. Wasn't that Sam Shepherd emerging from his office at last and running in the same direction? Were they all still in danger, she wondered, or had the ride simply returned to normal?

Alex gripped the sides of his seat. Was the ride going too fast? Could it come off its tracks and hurl them all into space? For the first time he was scared, and looking round he saw the others were as petrified as he was. Ben, wild-eyed and frozen, sat next to Emily who was screaming but not with excitement. Next to him, Kate seemed transfixed, droplets of sweat starting out on her forehead.

'Stop,' yelled the woman behind them. 'Stop!'

But the ride went even faster, roaring down the descents and pulling up the slopes with incredible force.

Only the child in the next car seemed to be enjoying it. 'This is great!' he shouted out to his terrified mother.

Ben suddenly closed his eyes and turned a strange shade of yellow.

The White Knuckle Ride hurtled past the control room and then seemed to pick up even more speed, even more power. Then, on top of the gradient, it shuddered to a halt again.

'This is ridiculous,' moaned Ben.

'I'll sue them,' said the woman.

'When's it starting up again, Mum?' asked the child.

As if in answer to his request, they began to move, but this time more slowly. Eventually the ride came to a stop by the control room, juddering slightly, as if it was playing with them and could rocket off again at any moment.

· 2 ·

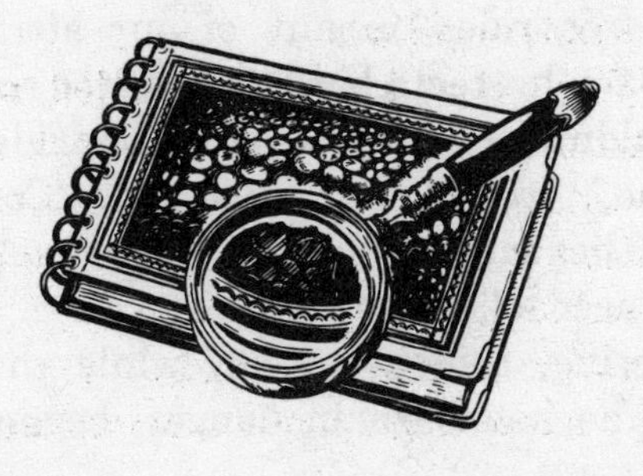

For a second, the passengers remained where they were, not daring to move, but eventually Ben stood up and stumbled from the car, the fairground revolving around him.

A small crowd of people had gathered, sensing something was wrong, pressing forward to see what was happening.

'I'm very sorry, ladies and gentlemen, boys and girls.' Sam Shepherd made a desperate attempt at jollity, but his normally florid face was ashen. 'There's been a technical hitch.'

'Hitch,' shouted the woman. 'You nearly killed us.'

'I can assure you—'

'You can assure me of nothing,' she yelled.

'All money will be refunded.'

'*That's* not good enough.'

'And free rides on any of our attractions,' added Sam, his teeth bared in a forced smile.

'I wouldn't go on any of your other rides if you paid me,' scoffed her husband. 'Come on, Madge,' he said, grabbing her arm, 'let's go home. I need a lie down.'

Muttering, they went off, while the child, sensing he had been in danger, began to cry again.

'You don't get these problems at Bill Buxton's Pleasure Park,' his mother shouted angrily. 'We'll be going there in future.'

Sam Shepherd's face crumpled. He was not only an ex-fisherman but an ex-boxer who had taken on all comers in the local pubs when he was younger, but now he was seeing his entire future crumbling away. As he sadly put a TEMPORARILY CLOSED sign at the entrance to the ride Kate felt desperately sorry for him. There was something vulnerable about Sam Shepherd – as if he was a hurt child, his toys attacked by a bully.

'You all right, Uncle?' asked Alex, but he didn't reply.

Cliff came out of the control room, looking concerned and angry. 'Someone's been messing about with the computer. Been doing a bit of reprogramming.'

'Who'd do that?' growled Sam as the crowd continued to gather. Then he said, 'Don't tell me. It must be Jud Tanner.'

'You can't jump to conclusions just like that. You've got no evidence.'

'I don't need any.'

'That's not fair—'

'I sacked Jud, didn't I? I sacked him for being a lazy little—' Sam paused. 'So he's taken his revenge, just like he told me he would. Right to my face he said, "I'll get you for this." Now he's tried to damage my business, terrify my punters and put them in danger.'

'You've still got no evidence,' remonstrated Cliff, and Kate looked at him approvingly. She admired his attitude, standing up to his boss, determined to give this Jud a chance.

'I told you – I don't need any.' Sam Shepherd turned to Alex. 'You know Jud?'

'A bit—'

'You seen him in the control room while Cliff

took his tea-break?'

'No.'

'You sure?'

'Sure, I'm sure.' Alex was indignant. 'I don't think we should discuss it out here – not with all these people around.'

'He's right,' said Cliff, looking round unhappily, and Ben realized, yet again, how close Tremarons were. Alex and Cliff were almost like brothers.

'OK. We'll go in my office and talk it through. Just you and me and my nephew.'

'No way,' said Alex. 'The other three are coming too.'

'What for?' asked Sam, annoyed.

'We solve mysteries. All four of us together,' Alex said casually, quite recovered from his alarming experiences. 'Remember Bloodhound Island? The Shadow Caves?'

'Yes,' said Kate, wishing she had brought her case book with her. 'We'll have a go at solving this for you.'

'I don't want amateur kids,' blustered Sam impatiently. 'Who do you think you are? The Five Finder Outers? The Secret Seven?'

'You've got the numbers wrong,' said Ben, feeling better now that the nausea had left him at last.

'I think they should join us.' Cliff was adamant. 'They could be useful.'

'All right,' sighed Sam. 'The more the merrier then.'

The walls of the caravan were covered with pictures of fairgrounds, some old, some new, and there were close-ups of roundabouts, dozens of them, mostly with the most beautifully carved and painted wooden horses.

The furnishings were strictly practical – a large bed, a bookcase, a small kitchen stove, a TV set and a chair.

'Since Ethel died – I've been alone,' he explained for Ben and Kate's benefit. 'We didn't have any kids.' He looked around at the pictures. 'Guess I'm married to the fairground now. I always hankered after being a showman, ever since I was a kid. Unlike young Alex here, I never wanted to go on the boats, but my mum and dad insisted. When Ethel died though – and left me a bit of money – I got to thinking I'd like to make a dream come true.' Despite his former aggression, Sam Shepherd had become much warmer and more expansive. 'I leased some new rides and the punters have been coming in quite nicely,' he continued. 'But now we're in dead trouble.'

'Why did you sack Jud?' asked Emily, trying to test out how co-operative Sam was going to be with them.

'I told you. He was lazy. Work shy. Directly Cliff showed up I could see who was the better worker. Not saying I didn't like Jud though.'

'I went to school with him,' said Cliff. 'Never had much confidence, that was Jud's problem.'

'*Was* he work shy?' asked Kate.

Cliff didn't answer directly. 'He didn't seem with you half the time. It was as if he was afraid of something.'

'Or someone,' snapped Sam. 'Like Buxton. Maybe *he's* behind all this.'

'How?' asked Ben, but Sam Shepherd only shrugged.

'I don't reckon Jud had anything to do with it.' Cliff was clearly determined to support him. 'As for Bill Buxton – he's a well-known villain. He could be up to anything.'

'Were you and Jud close?' asked Kate curiously.

'No. He didn't say much, just read a lot. Mainly comics. He was backward at school and used to get bullied. He can't look after himself.'

Cliff makes him sound a right wimp, thought Ben.

'Maybe Buxton put the screws on Jud,' said

Sam Shepherd, determined to make the connection somehow. 'That's a possibility, Cliff, and you know it. You liked the guy and so did I, that's why I trained him up on that computer, but he lacked your drive.'

'Where is he now then?' asked Alex. 'I haven't seen him around recently.'

'He still lives with his mum,' replied Sam. 'But he's probably done a runner. I'd better go and check that ride, find out what virus he's put in that computer.' He turned back to Cliff. 'I admire your loyalty, old son, but I've got a bet on with myself that I'm right about Jud.'

'Aren't you going to call the police then?' asked Kate, trying to push him a bit further.

Sam Shepherd shrugged irritably. 'How can I? Cliff's right. We haven't got any evidence. But I tell you what I *am* going to do. I'm going to watch this place day and night. No one's going to rubbish *my* fairground.'

Cliff nodded. 'We're going to make a stand against whoever it is – and we're going to win.'

No wonder Sam Shepherd trusts him, thought Kate. Cliff was so loyal, so much like Alex in his stubborn support.

3

Ben, Kate, Alex and Emily hurried back to Marlow House, the hotel that was constructed from four old fishermen's cottages and stood on the quayside at Tremaron, overlooking the harbour. Mr and Mrs Lewis had bought the old place, restoring it lovingly, hoping their guests would appreciate the wild Cornish coast.

There was a spare room in the Lewises' flat where officially Kate and Ben did their homework. Unofficially, it was a headquarters for mystery solving, where Kate kept her case book in a locked drawer.

Once they were sitting round the table, Kate said, 'There's another piece in the jigsaw puzzle. Jenny Rowe.'

'Who's Jenny Rowe?' demanded Alex.

'A guest. Mum told us she's applying for a job as cashier at the fairground. She's staying here until she gets digs, or at least that's what she says, but Mum thinks she's run away from home.'

'Come on,' said Emily. 'That's not good enough. Just because this Jenny Rowe wants to work at the fairground doesn't mean she's mixed up in the sabotage. It's a ridiculous idea.'

'Bertha says she's up to no good.'

Alex and Emily burst out laughing. Bertha, who helped Mrs Lewis in the kitchen at Marlow House, was regarded as one of the biggest gossips in Tremaron.

Kate looked down at her case book sadly. She had written:

THE MYSTERY OF
THE WHITE KNUCKLE RIDE

SUSPECTS:

JUD TANNER

But the rest of the page was painfully blank. What was even worse, Alex and Emily were laughing at her.

'Can't we go and check out Jud?' asked Ben, trying to come to her rescue.

'What are you going to do? March round to his house and ask him if he sabotaged that computer?' Alex was still grinning in the most irritating way possible.

There was a long silence during which Kate smouldered with anger. What right did Alex and Emily have to be so superior? Why couldn't they show a bit more enthusiasm? If there wasn't much to go on at the moment then couldn't they have a few ideas? Of course, she thought, even more angrily, they were Tremarons, weren't they? Stuck in their ways.

'Maybe you're right,' sighed Ben, suddenly traitorous. 'And Jenny probably *is* just a red herring.'

'Now how can you prove that?' grinned Emily.

'Prove what?'

'That she's a red herring. Is she covered in scales? Does she have a tail? Is she slippery?'

Alex sniggered, and Ben looked hurt, but Kate was too furious with her brother to be sympathetic. He must be getting a touch of the Tremarons too.

After supper, while Ben was watching TV, Kate

pleaded a headache and went to her bedroom. Then making sure she wasn't seen, she crept down the stairs and hurried out of the back door of Marlow House.

She arrived outside the fairground just as it was getting dark. The blaze of lights, the canned music and the smell of hot dogs mixed curiously with the smell of the sea. The White Knuckle Ride stood silent, the large notice still proclaiming: TEMPORARILY CLOSED.

Kate hung around for a while, trying to work out how secure the fairground actually was. A security fence ringed most of its boundary, but the southern-most side backed on to a low, sloping cliff that ran down to the beach. That was a possible way of getting in unobserved, she thought.

Then a question came into Kate's mind – a question that wouldn't go away. Was the ride closed when Cliff was having his lunch? If so, why hadn't he locked up the control room?

There's no time like the present, she told herself, even if the others weren't here. Anyway, it would serve them right for being so irritatingly smug and superior.

Kate knocked on the door.

'Come in.' His voice was abrupt.

As she walked into the control room, she could see Cliff sitting behind a computer display, hunched and exhausted. Somehow he looked different, much less vigorous. In fact he seemed slightly defeated.

'It's the girl detective,' he grinned, making a painful attempt at humour as if to force himself back into character. It gave her a curious feeling.

'I forgot to ask a question,' she said self-consciously.

'That's not very professional, is it? Not good police procedure.' Now he was back in his more confident mode again.

'I don't know about that.' Kate was firm. 'Even the police must slip up sometimes.' She paused and then asked, 'Whoever reprogrammed the computer would have to know it pretty well, wouldn't they? I mean – some stranger couldn't just walk in and know what to do.'

'It would have to be someone who understood the program,' Cliff agreed quietly.

'And that leaves you and Jud.'

'Yes.' He spoke without expression.

'Anyone else?'

'There's Sam. But I don't see him sabotaging his own ride.'

Kate was surprised at how frankly Cliff was

speaking to her. He seemed to be taking her seriously now. But it all felt too easy and she couldn't work out why.

There was an uneasy silence. Then Cliff said, 'I thought you wanted to ask me a question.'

'I – we – forgot to ask if you close the ride while you have your lunch.'

'Jud and I used to work in shifts. But since I've been on my own, I've just put the sign up for a few minutes while I grab a sandwich. Sam's got an advert in the local paper – so maybe we can train up someone fast.'

'Do you lock up the control room when you go out?'

'Of course.' He suddenly looked anxious and then muttered, 'I might have forgotten once or twice.' There was a slightly uncomfortable pause. 'Now if you've finished the inquisition, perhaps you'll let me get on.' Then he grinned again to take away the slight tinge of hostility. 'Where's your notebook? Aren't all private detectives meant to carry one?'

'I've got my case book at home. I commit everything to memory and then write up my notes.' Kate knew she sounded absurdly pompous.

'We all make mistakes you know,' replied Cliff. 'Occasionally.'

She knew he was referring to the unlocked control room.

'Oh yes.' She was brisk. 'Of course we do. We always regret them, though,' Kate added.

4

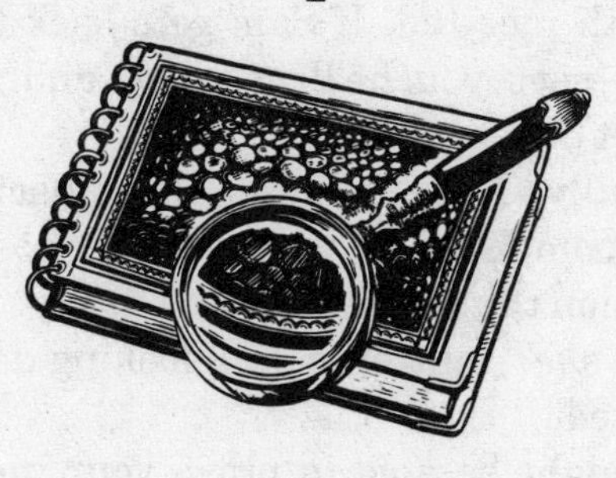

'What's going on?' Cliff jumped to his feet as the sound of swearing and shouting began outside. 'You stay where you are,' he said brusquely, as he pushed past Kate.

She had no intention of doing anything of the kind, and followed Cliff out, standing on the steps of the control room and watching him wade into a group of young thugs who were kicking a figure lying on the ground. Directly he intervened they ran off, laughing, and Cliff gently helped their victim to his feet. He was young and thin, with a small frame, and his hair was so short that it looked like fur.

'They're not Tremarons,' said an old lady with dark, wizened features whom Kate recognized as the owner of the Hoopla stall.

'You're right, Sal,' said Cliff. 'You'd better come with me, Jud. If Sam gets back from the pub and sees you he'll go crazy and you just might get done-over again.'

Hopefully, Kate followed them back to the control room, but Cliff was no longer hospitable.

'Question time's over,' he said firmly.

'Who's *she*?' muttered Jud, looking dazed and bewildered.

'She might be able to prove your innocence.' Cliff grinned. 'Kate's a detective,' he said mockingly. 'The White Knuckle went bananas with a load of punters on it this afternoon. We could have had a nasty accident.'

'It *can't* go bananas.'

'Someone reprogrammed the computer. Unfortunately, Sam thinks you're the someone.'

'Why should I do a terrible thing like that?'

'Sam reckons you want revenge.'

Jud was shaking now, his thin shoulders hunched, and he slumped into a chair. 'I swear I didn't. I wouldn't put people's lives at risk like that.' Then Jud gazed up at Cliff. 'Do *you* think I did it?' he demanded.

'Of course I don't. It's not in your nature,' Cliff said firmly. 'Sam doesn't agree though.'

'No – he wouldn't. But he's not exactly a student of human nature, is he?' Jud was indignant now.

'This business is hard and you know it. Especially with Buxton breathing down his neck.'

'Sam Shepherd not only thinks you did it, but that Buxton *got* you to do it,' said Kate crisply. 'There doesn't seem to be a shred of proof though.'

'How old are you?' asked Jud incredulously.

'Eleven.'

'You're pretty together for eleven, aren't you?'

Kate smiled. 'We've already solved a couple of mysteries. Haven't you heard of Bloodhound—'

'All right,' said Cliff. 'Don't let's go for a wander down memory lane. Sam could be here any minute, and if he sees Jud he might just call the police and that could get nasty.'

'Let him,' replied Jud. 'I've got nothing to hide and the kid's right – he's got no proof.'

'How come that bunch attacked you? And what were you doing here anyway? You and Sam didn't exactly part on good terms.'

'He said I was lazy.' Jud was very resentful. 'He'd no idea how hard I worked, how much extra time I put in. I was angry – so would anyone have been – but I'd never sabotage anything. You know that. Anyway, I overheard that bunch in the pub,' he continued. 'They were talking about doing the fairground over. I thought they were just joking at first, but I could see Sam in the other bar and I thought I should tell him. Of course he'd had a skinful as usual, and when I went across to him he started shouting at me something rotten. Then I saw the thugs leave and I followed them here. I didn't know what to do.'

'You could have called the police,' said Cliff.

'I didn't know whether they meant what they were saying or just joking, but directly they got inside the fairground they started looking for trouble. I was sure they were going to do some damage so I challenged them.'

'Just you? Why didn't you give me a shout?' Cliff was amazed.

'I wasn't sure of my welcome,' he admitted sadly. 'So thanks for coming out when you did, Cliff.' Jud also glanced at Kate gratefully. 'What's your name?'

'Kate Lewis.'

'What makes you believe in me?' he asked her.

'Because Cliff does,' she replied evasively.

Jud looked at her for a moment then he turned to Cliff and said, 'I'd better be on my way. Before Sam shows up.'

'Wait a minute – do you think Buxton set up that gang too?' asked Cliff. 'If so, he's running a pretty fierce campaign, isn't he?'

'You know what a villain he is. He'll just push Sam until he topples over.'

'We're getting tighter security tomorrow,' said Cliff. 'Sam's moving the cash kiosk up by the gate and he's going to install a phone and a panic button.' He paused. 'He's just employed a girl to work in it.'

'Who's that?' asked Jud, gingerly feeling a lump that was coming up under his eye.

'Name of Jenny Rowe.'

'She's come down from Plymouth,' said Kate. 'Mum thinks she's run away from somewhere.'

'Tremaron's having an invasion,' Jud grinned weakly. 'They don't like strangers here.' Then he stiffened. 'I suppose—' His voice died away.

'You suppose what?'

'She couldn't be a Buxton plant, could she? To cause trouble inside.'

'Don't be so daft,' said Cliff. 'He may be running a campaign against us, but he's not that clever.'

*

Jud and Kate hurried away from the fairground together. 'You're sure you're OK?' she asked as they passed the harbour wall.

'I'm fine.' He paused. 'Thanks for believing in me.' He looked very young in the half-light – young and vulnerable.

'Cliff believes in you most of all,' she said carefully, feeling horrible inside. Kate would have liked to trust him, but how could she?

'There's no proof either way – like you said.' Jud shrugged and she suddenly liked him, particularly for his honesty.

'What are you going to do now?' she asked.

'Maybe I'll just clear off. Find some work in Padstow.'

'If you do that,' said Kate quietly, 'it *will* look as if you're guilty.'

Jud frowned, but his eyes betrayed his fear. 'So what should I do? Hang around? As I'm prime suspect I'll be nicked if there's any more sabotage.'

'It'll only look worse if you run,' persisted Kate.

'Maybe you're right. I'll stay at home then. Get under Mum's feet. That'll be like a prison sentence in itself.'

· 5 ·

Ben was indignant when he caught his sister creeping up the stairs that night. 'You shouldn't have gone out on your own.'

'I had to kick-start this mystery. No one else wanted to know.'

'What happened then?' he asked impatiently.

Kate gave him an infuriating smile. 'I'll tell you tomorrow morning,' she said. 'Better give the others a ring and ask them to come over.' She continued up the stairs to bed, knowing she was punishing him but too tired to be merciful.

Next morning, when Kate had finished explaining, Alex apologized. 'I'm sorry we doubted you,' he said.

'You mustn't take that kind of risk again,' said Emily. Clearly, she was sorry too. 'We're all in this together. Right, Alex?'

Alex nodded. 'What's the next move then?' he said.

'Jenny Rowe?' asked Kate uncertainly, remembering how they'd all laughed at her before about suspecting Jenny.

'She's having a late breakfast in the dining-room,' Ben replied. 'But we can't *all* go down there.'

'Your turn to take the initiative,' said Kate sweetly, and Ben realized his sister hadn't quite forgiven him yet.

He glanced at Alex and Emily doubtfully.

'It's your hotel,' said Emily.

Ben cleared his throat uncertainly. Interviewing Jenny Rowe wasn't a job he was exactly burning to do. 'I'll go and tell Bertha I'll give her a hand clearing the tables. Mum's out at the shops, thank goodness.'

'Bertha *will* be amazed,' said Kate.

'Why?'

'We get paid to clear the tables. You've never done it for free before.'

Ben smiled weakly. 'I'll tell her I'm in a generous mood.'

Jenny Rowe was a tall girl with cropped auburn hair and a pensive expression. She was buttering toast as Ben arrived.

'Don't mind if I clear, do you?' he asked nervously.

'I don't mind,' she said, looking up at him curiously. 'But the lady's already done most of it.'

'Sorry.' Too late Ben noticed she was right. What was more, the other tables were also cleared too and Jenny Rowe was the last person in the room. 'Can I take the teapot?' he muttered.

'I'm still using it.'

'The hot water jug?'

'I'm still using that too.' Her voice was flat, but he wondered if he could detect a flicker of amusement in her eyes, or could it be hostility?

'The salt cellar?' he asked desperately.

'Third time lucky. You can take that. But it doesn't seem worth making a journey for, does it?'

'Er. No. Not really. No.' Ben was becoming

really flustered now.

'You're not trying to chat me up, are you?' She gave him the hint of a mocking smile.

'Me?'

'Why not?'

'Oh well,' said Ben. 'I'll get on then.' He walked across the room, knowing he had failed. Then he decided to take a last-minute risk. 'I hear you got yourself a job at the fairground,' he began awkwardly.

'Yes.'

'I hope you enjoy it.'

'I need the money.'

'Sam Shepherd is our friend's uncle. He's a good boss.'

'That's nice. He seems to spend a lot of time in the pub though, doesn't he?' She finished the last piece of toast. 'Want a plate?'

'Plate?'

'You're clearing, aren't you?'

'Oh yes. Thanks. He's er – Sam's had some bad luck recently.' Ben could hear himself blundering on.

'Who?' Jenny Rowe was really making life difficult for Ben now, and he still couldn't tell whether she was laughing at him or if she was angry.

'Sam Shepherd. We were on the White

Knuckle Ride and it broke down at the top.'

'Yes?'

'I think it's still closed.'

'Yes?'

'Oh well – better get on then.'

'Why don't you?' Jenny Rowe yawned and Ben beat a hasty retreat to the kitchen.

To make up for his disastrous failure with Jenny, Ben decided to cross-examine Bertha. He found her clattering the washing up in the kitchen, singing loudly and gazing out of the window. Bertha was in her sixties now and had already brought up a large family. She was a bustling, determined woman, and her job at Marlow House had been a blessing to all concerned. Bertha was Mum's right hand, capable of amazing amounts of sheer hard work. She also made it her own personal business to find out as much as she could about the guests.

'She's a bit jumpy, isn't she?' Ben knew he had been the jumpy one. 'She was really short.'

'Short?'

'Jenny Rowe.'

'She's quite tall, isn't she?'

Ben closed his eyes. Surely he wasn't going to have yet another difficult conversation. What was the matter with him? Had he lost his touch?

Kate would have made a much better job of all this.

'I mean she was bad-tempered.'

'She's secretive, that one is.' Bertha scoured a pan vigorously.

'I thought that's what Tremarons were.'

'What was that?' She always took offence at any criticism of the town. Why hadn't he remembered?

Ben hurried on, trying to make a success out of another disaster. 'She was really rude.'

'Were you poking your nose in then?'

'I wouldn't do that,' Ben replied anxiously.

Bertha suddenly smiled and took her hands out of the soapy water, drying them on a towel. 'You're right though. She's a sulky miss. But there'll be a reason why.' Her voice was low and full of meaning, and he could sense now that she wanted to pass on what she knew. Ben felt a wave of relief. Maybe he could salvage something after all.

'A reason why?' he repeated tentatively.

'Wouldn't mind betting there's trouble at home,' Bertha said grimly. 'Could be she's run away from her parents. She wouldn't open up to me when thousands would, and I know how worried your mum is. I mean – why does Jenny Rowe carry all that cash on her and then say she must have a job as she needs the money?' Bertha lowered her voice to a whisper. 'She opened her purse and it was stuffed full of fifty-pound notes. Now where would she get those from?'

'What do you reckon, Bertha?' Ben was hanging on to her every word.

She paused and gave an indrawn breath. 'Of course I can't be sure, but I reckon she's gone and run away from home, taken her mother's life savings.' There was a pregnant pause which Ben knew he mustn't fill. 'What's more,' Bertha lowered her voice still further and gazed around the kitchen as if Jenny Rowe had slipped in unnoticed and hidden herself under the table, 'she keeps bad company.'

'Where?'

'The Man of War.'

Ben knew the pub. The few trouble-making youngsters in the town drank there, as well as some older men who were usually out of work, occasionally making a slender living selling hot dogs and ice-cream.

'How do you know?'

'I happened to see her through the window.' Bertha sniffed. 'She wasn't alone.' She paused, waiting for him to ask the obvious question and Ben rapidly obliged.

'Who was she with?'

'I couldn't see his face. A young man.'

'Can you describe him?'

Bertha gazed at him intently. 'Very slight he was. Skinhead. Narrow shoulders. Not her type at all.'

Kate wrote the second suspect under Jud Tanner's name in her case book with some relish. She felt like saying, 'I told you so,' but managed to restrain herself.

JENNY ROWE.

'We should recruit Bertha into the club,' said Alex. 'She's brilliant on surveillance.'

'We'll keep her as our leg woman,' replied Ben firmly. 'She could be wrong though.'

'It looks as if Jenny went out for a drink with Jud. Why shouldn't she, I suppose. But what a place to drink in,' said Emily disapprovingly.

'The Man of War's a real dump.' Alex was indignant. 'The police should do something about that place. It lets Tremaron down.'

'Do you think Bill Buxton goes there?' asked Kate. 'I know he's not local but—'

'If he wanted to recruit some crooks,' said Emily. 'That would be the place.'

'To sum it all up so far,' began Ben. 'Jud could be in league with Buxton and sabotaged the computer. Now Buxton needs another insider because Jud's under suspicion. Who better than runaway Jenny?'

'She seems to have plenty of money if Bertha's right,' pointed out Alex.

'Buxton could just have given her an advance,' said Kate.

'Suppose those thugs were working for Buxton too,' suggested Emily. 'Perhaps they *were* giving Jud a work-over to stop him grassing?'

Kate sighed. 'He seemed so defenceless. He was really convincing.'

'He was just putting on a little boy lost act,' said Ben brutally.

'Cliff believes he's innocent.'

'I've known Cliff for years, and he's a good guy,' said Alex. 'He wouldn't want to condemn anyone. Anyway, it's all circumstantial, isn't it? Just the way things look. We need hard evidence.'

'It's not going to be easy to get it,' said Kate, 'unless—'

'Unless what?' asked Emily impatiently.

'Unless we keep the fairground under surveillance.' Kate looked grim. 'I'm sure the sabotage isn't over yet.'

·6·

They had decided to take it in turns to keep an eye on the fairground for the rest of the day. While Ben and Kate and Emily played cards in the spare room, Alex had gone to take his shift. About eleven, he telephoned Kate. 'Something weird's happened. Uncle Sam's re-employed Jud.' He sounded amazed.

Kate was also shaken. 'Why on earth's he done that?'

'Cliff told him that Jud tried to protect the fairground last night. Uncle Sam thinks a lot of Cliff. Somehow he managed to convince him. Unless—'

'Unless what?'

'Unless he thinks it's easier to have Jud where he can keep an eye on him. Maybe catch him before he does some more damage.'

'That's a possibility,' Kate agreed. 'If so, then your Uncle Sam's cleverer than we thought. But he's taking a risk.'

'What do we do next then?'

'Step up the surveillance. We'll all come down.'

'That could get expensive,' Alex replied.

It did. Kate, Ben, Alex and Emily spent a fortune, despite the fact that they tried to stay off the rides and keep to the slot machines and side shows. There was, however, a limit to the number of times they could play hoopla, and eventually old Sal demanded, 'You got money to burn, you kids? This is your sixth go and you haven't won a prize yet. I'd give up if I were you.'

They did, playing the slot machines and changing money with Jenny Rowe who gave them a brief smile and then ignored them for the rest of the morning. She seemed quite at home in the kiosk, which had now been moved to the entrance to the fairground.

'We can't go on like this,' said Alex, desperately trying to manipulate a miniature crane whose mechanical claw reached down towards cheap prizes in a plastic dome. Try as he might, he couldn't get the crane's grab to contact with any of them. 'I'm broke,' he said miserably.

'So am I,' said Emily.

Kate looked at her watch. 'It's almost lunch-time. Let's just wait to see where Jenny Rowe goes in her break.'

As she spoke, Jud Tanner emerged from the control room and strolled towards them. He looked much more relaxed and confident. 'As you can see, the boss had a change of heart. So Cliff and I can work regular shifts now.' He looked around him. 'It's great to be back but I'm keeping my eyes peeled.'

Did he realize he was still under suspicion, wondered Ben, or was he playing some kind of waiting game? 'Do you think there'll be any more sabotage?' he asked innocently.

'Could be. Buxton's a ruthless man. If he's behind all this, he won't give up yet. I reckon he wants Mr Shepherd out of business – like fast.'

'Did you find out what went wrong with the

computer?' asked Alex.

'Reprogrammed – and in such a way that it's been difficult to get right. But Cliff and I managed it in the end. The White Knuckle should be back in action this afternoon after we've run a few more tests.'

'Do you know Jenny Rowe – the new cashier?' asked Kate. 'She's staying with us.'

'I met her in a pub.' He didn't seem in the least put out. 'Bust up with her boyfriend in Plymouth and came down to Tremaron for a breather. So I'm in there with a chance.' He glanced at the kiosk. 'I didn't think she'd look at me at first but we're going for lunch together today.' Jud shrugged his thin shoulders. 'Probably won't last though.'

'Where are you going to take her?' Ben asked cunningly.

'Down the Tudor Café. Last time we went to the Man of War. Never again. It's a right dump. Better get back now.' He turned towards the control room. 'I've got to be on my best behaviour around here.'

'He's up to something,' said Emily when the door had closed.

'Or maybe he just wants to make a go of things,' snapped Kate.

'Why are you defending him?' said Emily

crossly. 'You're always able to look at both sides of a picture. You don't seem able to do that with Jud though, do you?'

· 7 ·

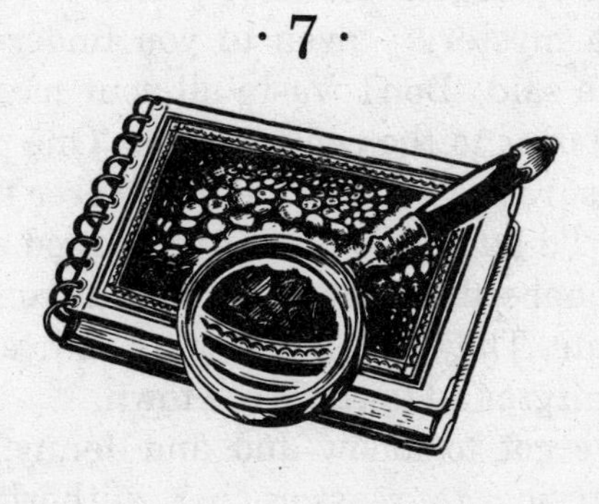

'Got us under surveillance, have you?' chuckled Sam Shepherd as he lumbered out of his caravan, looking falsely jovial. If only he knew how right he was, thought Ben.

'You trust Jud now, do you?' Alex asked his uncle.

Sam Shepherd shrugged and passed a hand over his eyes. 'I wouldn't say that, but I'd rather have him working for me than against me, if you see what I mean. Anyway, I'm going to give him the benefit of the doubt. Cliff believes in him so maybe I should.'

'But you don't,' said Alex bleakly.

'Don't you start telling me what I think,' growled Sam, taking the sting out of the words with an apologetic smile. 'I prefer to remain a bit of a mystery – even to you finder-outers.' Then he said, 'Don't waste all your money.' He strolled over to the control room. 'One person I *can* trust round here is Cliff. If it weren't for him I think I'd pack this place up for good and all.' Sam Shepherd sounded as if he was completely desperate. They watched him as he headed out of the fairground towards the town.

'We've got to follow Jud and Jenny,' hissed Kate, trying to reassert her authority after Emily's attack on her.

'All of us?' Emily looked round warily. 'Don't you think we're a bit of a crowd?'

'OK,' said Ben. 'You and Alex go. Kate and I've been doing the leg work so far. But be careful – don't let them see you.'

'What do you think we're going to do?' asked Alex. 'Go down to the Tudor Café and sit at their table?'

'That might speed things up,' said Emily. 'We could ask them if they plan any more sabotage this afternoon.'

Leaving Ben and Kate to spend what little money they had left on the slot machines, Alex and Emily set off, strolling casually out of the fairground and up the narrow street outside, feeling increasingly nervous.

It wasn't long before Emily whispered, 'There they are. Just turning into the café. Let's give them a minute and then try to see through the window.'

'What then?' asked Alex.

'Make sure neither of them leaves,' she said. 'They could easily give us the slip in the back streets if we're not careful.'

'This isn't New York,' he protested. 'They're not gangsters.'

'No,' Emily replied, 'it's Tremaron – and it's full of alleys. That's why we want to keep them both pinned down.'

Cautiously, they strolled past the Tudor Café, but the windows were partly misted up and they couldn't see in. Turning back, Emily and Alex approached the place again, this time pausing to gaze at the menu. As they studied it in detail, Emily elbowed Alex so hard in the stomach that he gasped in pain.

'Jenny's gone,' she hissed.

As they both peered through the misty glass,

Alex could see that Jud was sitting alone at a table.

'She might be in the toilet.'

'Keep your voice down.' They moved from the doorway to the front window where they both remained, self-consciously staring into the interior of the darkly panelled café.

They must have waited for over five minutes, but there was still no sign of Jenny Rowe returning to her seat.

'She's been gone an awful long time,' muttered Alex.

They continued to gaze through the window, but there was still no sign of Jenny and one of the waitresses began to give them both a glacial smile.

'Let's get back,' said Alex.

'This crane doesn't pick up a thing.' Ben worked the grab in the glass dome with mounting frustration. 'It's a con.'

'We haven't got any more money,' began Kate and then paused. 'Did you see that?'

'See what?'

'I thought I saw someone running out of the Hall of Mirrors.'

'A man? A woman?' Ben asked impatiently.

'It was more like a shadow.'

'Wishful thinking.' He was staring at the miniature crane in mounting fury.

'There *was* someone there,' Kate insisted as Alex and Emily came running up to them, flustered and breathless.

'Jenny's disappeared,' gasped Alex. 'Only Jud's in the café.'

'I saw a figure running out of the Hall of Mirrors. At least I thought I did.' She couldn't be sure now and felt foolish, as if she was letting everyone down by imagining things.

'Which way did they go?' demanded Emily impatiently.

'It was too quick—'

But Alex was already running out of the fairground again, back down the road towards the café, leaving the other three to gaze at each other uneasily.

Ben was the first to see the little bright dart of flame.

For a few seconds all three of them stared at the Hall of Mirrors as if they were in a hypnotic trance, not really believing what they had just seen, and then they began to run towards the building. As they did so, Alex returned, yelling breathlessly, 'She's in the café again.'

Jenny must have run amazingly fast, thought Ben.

'Raise the alarm,' shouted Kate.

There was now a gathering cloud of smoke billowing out of the building, and Alex ran to the kiosk where the woman who was normally in charge of the coconut shy had taken over.

'Call the fire brigade,' he gasped. 'The Hall of Mirrors is on fire.'

· 8 ·

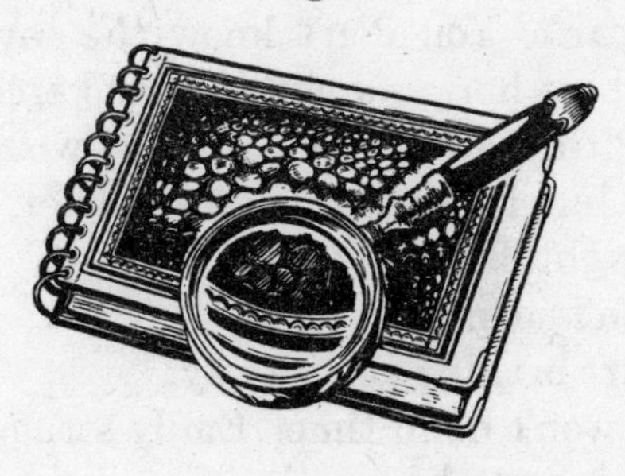

'Is there anyone in there?' yelled Cliff as he ran out of the control room. 'There shouldn't be.'

'Why not?' asked Ben.

'It's closed for cleaning. There should be a sign.'

As they both ran toward the fire, Cliff picked up a battered placard bearing the words TEMPORARILY CLOSED FOR CLEANING which had been lying face down on the ground. Meanwhile, the smoke and flames were increasing and there was a terrifying crackling noise from inside.

'Is anyone there?' yelled Kate. 'Anyone inside?'

Very faintly they heard a choking cry.

'I'm going in,' said Cliff.

'I'm coming with you.' Emily was determined.

'You can't. You don't know the layout.' He pushed past her, and with a handkerchief over his mouth ran inside. Emily would have followed him if Ben hadn't grabbed her.

'He's right. If you get lost in there—'

'He can't go in alone!'

'The fire brigade's on its way.'

'They won't be in time!' Emily struggled, but Ben clung on to her as they heard the sound of breaking glass.

After what seemed an eternity, Cliff struggled out of the smoke carrying a young boy who was choking and spluttering and gasping for breath.

'Anyone else in there?' yelled Alex.

'No. I checked.' Cliff laid the boy down on the ground as the now familiar crowd began to gather. 'The kid's not too bad. I found him crouched in a corner.' Cliff was coughing badly and there was a burn on his wrist.

'What the hell's going on?' Sam Shepherd had reached them now and Jud Tanner and Jenny

Rowe were running into the fairground. Kate could smell beer on Sam's breath so it was obvious where he had been, but Jud and Jenny's arrival seemed unnaturally fast to her. The explanation, however, was not long in coming.

'The waitress told us she could see smoke,' said Jenny.

Emily watched her closely, but she seemed merely shocked and frightened – as anyone would be. Jud too looked shaken and was questioning Cliff.

By now the flames were licking the roof of the Hall of Mirrors and the blaze, accompanied by the sound of shattering glass, was already well out of control.

'The fire brigade's on the way,' said Alex.

'Then where the hell is it?' yelled Sam. 'They've only got to come from just outside town. Are you all right, son?' He leant over the boy who was already scrambling to his feet.

'I'm OK.'

'What's your name?' asked Cliff gently.

'Rob.'

'You shouldn't have gone in there. The sign said closed for cleaning.'

'There wasn't any sign,' said the boy, beginning to tremble with delayed shock.

'Of course there was,' snapped Cliff. 'I put it

there myself.'

'Why didn't the cleaner put the sign up?' asked Sam in surprise.

'The place was filthy. Mrs Tyler hadn't touched it for weeks, so when she came in I made it her first job and put up the notice. She wasn't best pleased.'

'I tell you there was no sign,' yelled Rob, getting agitated.

'Of course there was.' Cliff was adamant. 'But there's no point in arguing. We should get you to hospital.'

Alex had a sudden thought. The sign would have given someone the perfect chance to creep in and start the fire. Perhaps it had got knocked over as they sped out – as Jenny Rowe sped out? Alex knew there was a yard at the back of the Tudor Café that opened on to a narrow alley which wound down towards the fairground. Why hadn't he and Emily thought of that before?

As the sirens began to sound over Tremaron, the flames leapt through the roof of the Hall of Mirrors. Alex moved towards Jenny and Jud, sniffing cautiously. Kate watched him curiously. What on earth was he doing?

The crowd scattered as two fire engines and an ambulance swept into the fairground, past the kiosk and up to the blazing building.

'Casualty!' shouted Sam, and the paramedics ran towards Rob while a police car roared up behind them.

'Anyone still in there?' asked one of the firemen.

'No,' said Cliff. 'I checked the place out when I rescued this kid. It's clear.'

'Well, we'll have to check for ourselves.'

Cliff began to choke and at once one of the paramedics hurried over to him.

'You've inhaled smoke. You should come to the hospital too.'

'No chance,' began Cliff but Sam Shepherd immediately overruled him.

'Do what he says,' he growled. 'You're a hero, and don't anyone forget it.'

But as Cliff reluctantly walked over to the ambulance, Emily thought she smelt petrol.

· 9 ·

'Jenny Rowe would definitely have had time to get back to start that fire. Emily and I blew it. One of us should have kept an eye on the yard. Kate – you saw someone—' Alex was telling the other three what he had been trying to work out.

They had all withdrawn to the comparative shelter of the unstaffed coconut shy, while the firemen fought to get the flames under control, and the crowd, banished from the fairground, began to swell outside the gate.

'I just couldn't see who it was,' Kate insisted. She still felt guilty that she had not been sufficiently observant. '*Did* Jenny smell of petrol, Alex?'

He shook his head. 'Not that I could make out.'

'Maybe all that fishing has ruined your sense of smell,' suggested Emily.

'What about Jud?' asked Ben.

Alex shook his head. 'Besides, he would never have got from the café to the fairground in time. So that rules him out too.'

'There's only one curious thing,' said Emily slowly. 'Something I don't really understand.'

'What is it?' asked Ben impatiently.

'The only person who smelt of petrol round here was Cliff.'

There was a long, uneasy silence, eventually broken by Alex. 'There's a simple explanation for that,' he said at last. 'He must have run through some petrol that hadn't caught light. It was probably all over the floor.'

'We don't even know if petrol was used,' pointed out Kate.

'I don't suppose the person used fire lighters,' said Ben sarcastically.

The jets from the hoses were playing on the

flames that were still shooting through the roof of the Hall of Mirrors, but it was obviously too late to save the building which was now burning from end to end.

As the ambulance sped off with Cliff and Rob, Sam Shepherd joined them, his eyes full of tears. He looked completely broken.

'This is going to ruin me.'

'You're insured, aren't you?' asked Alex.

'I couldn't afford the highest premiums so they won't give me the full replacement value. I might as well close the place down now.'

'You've *got* to fight back.'

Alex began to tell his uncle about their suspicions, blurting it all out, his words tumbling over each other.

When he had finished, however, Sam Shepherd seemed shocked. 'Jenny Rowe? Working for Bill Buxton? I don't think so.'

'Why not? She disappeared from the café,' insisted Emily.

'I expect she was spending a penny.'

'For over seven minutes?'

'Well, yes, that does seem a long time,' Sam agreed.

'I thought I saw someone running out of the Hall of Mirrors,' added Kate.

'Could you identify them?'

'No.'

'You should tell the police. I'll ask them to speak to you. But as for Jenny, I know there's a rational explanation. Now if it had been Jud—'

'He was in the café all the time,' repeated Alex.

'Jenny!' Sam shouted. 'Step over here for a minute. Jud, you stay just where you are.'

Jud looked alarmed, but did as he was told.

'Jenny, now I don't want you to get upset,' began Sam.

'Upset?'

'These kids are amateur sleuths,' Sam said patronizingly. 'They've made a bit of a mistake I expect.'

'There's *no* mistake,' said Alex, but he suddenly sounded defensive and lacking in confidence.

'What *is* all this?' Jenny Rowe's voice was cold.

'They put you and Jud under surveillance.'

'They did *what*?' The anger gradually spread over her face.

'They took a peek at you when you were in the Tudor Café.' Even Sam was sounding a little embarrassed now.

'What for?' Jenny Rowe demanded, her anger and indignation rising.

What was she really thinking, wondered Emily. Was she on the level or just keeping up an elaborate front?

'The kids are trying to find out who's doing the sabotage round here. They think you might be working for Buxton—'

'Working for Buxton!' Jenny's face was scarlet with rage. 'How dare you involve me in your silly games. Pestering me at breakfast, and now spying—'

'You weren't at your table for at least seven minutes,' interrupted Alex.

'You think I was the saboteur?' Jenny's lips were twisted in a sardonic smile.

'Of course it's all nonsense, but what were you doing all that time?' said Sam.

'I should say it is.' Jenny turned to Alex. 'Well, my little private eyes, I have an alibi as they say.'

'What is it?'

'I was in the kitchen of the Tudor Café with Mrs Petrie. I'd met her when I had tea there a couple of days ago.'

'*Why* were you in the kitchen?' demanded Emily.

'Mrs Petrie was giving me some of her special recipes – ones she doesn't sell in the café,' Jenny explained curtly. 'She'll vouch for me – if that's necessary.'

There was a long silence, eventually broken by Alex. 'I see,' he said quietly.

There seemed nothing more to say.

The firemen were still damping down the burnt-out shell of the Hall of Mirrors an hour later, while Sam Shepherd looked on, his face grim.

Ben, Kate, Emily and Alex still hung around, feeling unwanted but somehow unable to leave the fairground which had now been closed to the public for the rest of the day. One of the police officers had spoken to Kate, but had gone away disappointed when she couldn't give him a description – or even confirm she had actually seen someone.

Jenny Rowe was back in the kiosk, sorting out the morning's takings and Jud was in the control room of the White Knuckle Ride, hunched over the computer.

Unable to bear the tension, Alex decided to apologize to his uncle. 'I'm sorry about that. I was obviously mistaken.'

'You were only trying to help,' said Sam Shepherd brokenly. 'But you've got to stop all this stuff now. It's only going to cause more trouble. So I don't want you lot prowling around looking for clues. You're very welcome to come into the fair, but no more investigating. And if I find you're at it again you won't be welcome here. Got it?'

'Got it,' said Alex miserably.

'That's it then,' Mrs Lewis proclaimed as the four of them hovered at the bottom of the stairs of Marlow House, hoping to go up to the spare room.

'What do you mean?' asked Kate defensively, and then realized that Jenny Rowe must have got to her mother first.

'Who do you think you are?' demanded Mum so loudly that they could see Bertha had come out of the kitchen and was listening avidly. 'The CID?'

'We solved two mysteries,' said Ben hopefully. 'Now we're on a third.'

'You're certainly not! Just because you stupidly plunged yourselves into danger and discovered some wrong-doing doesn't mean to say you can go on pretending to be detectives. Of course it's my fault and I should have spoken to you earlier, but it's got to stop, and now. I want you to make me a promise – all four of you – that this is the end of it, particularly since we've had a complaint from a guest.'

'Some guests haven't been all they should be,'

muttered Kate. She was determined not to make any promises and hoped the other three would stand firm. What would life be without mysteries to solve?

'I don't care what they were. Jenny Rowe certainly isn't a criminal, and it was dreadful to try and make her out to be one. You'll be seriously damaging our business here if you haven't done so already.'

'Anyone can make mistakes, Mum,' said Kate.

'That was one mistake too many,' Mrs Lewis countered fiercely, with Bertha's ears flapping in the background. 'Do you think I want our guests to think they're spied on all the time?'

Bertha's the real master spy, thought Ben rebelliously.

'Sorry, Mum,' they chorused while Alex and Emily remained tactfully silent.

Mrs Lewis looked at them all with deep suspicion. 'I don't want all of you plotting in that spare room either. There's only one reason for you two going in there – and that's to do your homework. Do you understand?'

'Yes,' said Kate. 'We understand, Mum.' All right, she was thinking. Drive us underground then.

· 10 ·

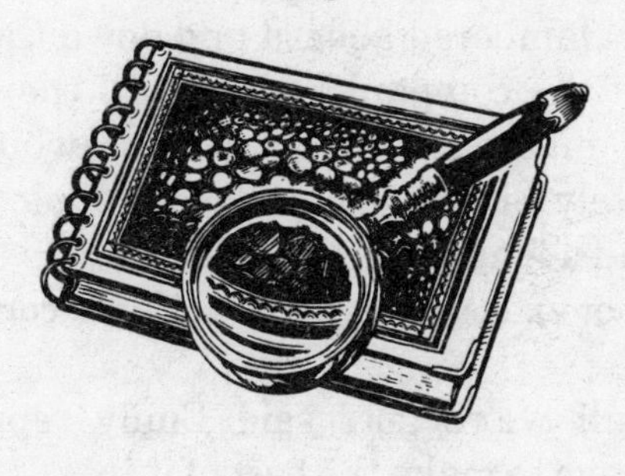

They stood by the harbour wall, watching the fishing boats being repaired on the slipway. It was five o'clock and the evening was sunny and warm as the tide began to run in.

'So where's underground?' asked Kate briskly, clutching her precious case book, rescued from their banned headquarters.

'What about the *Spindrift*. She's up on the mud and her owner abandoned her years ago,' suggested Alex.

The *Spindrift* sounded a possibility, and the four of them walked dejectedly round the harbour, up a narrow lane and then down again to the marsh where the hulk of the former sailing cruiser lay in the mud. Her mast and rigging had long since disappeared, but her hull was well clear of the tide line.

They clambered aboard and down the rotting steps of the companion-way until they arrived in a musty-smelling cabin, which was completely empty except for a couple of bunk beds and a long, scarred table.

'It's not exactly comfortable, is it?' complained Kate.

'It's all we've got,' said Emily reprovingly. 'We'll have to make the best of it.'

They sat down gloomily round the table as Kate opened her case book and read out the names of the suspects so far.

JUD TANNER

JENNY ROWE

'We should add Bill Buxton,' said Alex. 'I'm sure he's behind all this.'

'We've got no evidence of that,' pointed out Ben. 'And I've had another thought. You don't suppose your uncle could be doing it himself for the insurance money? I mean – it's a risky business running a fairground. Do you think he wants out?'

To everyone's surprise Alex wasn't offended but considered the situation carefully. 'I don't *think* he would. I know how much the fairground means to him. It's all he's got left in life.'

'I can see the sense of that,' said Kate. 'I don't reckon we *should* put him down as a suspect. What does everyone think?'

They all shook their heads, convinced now that Sam Shepherd was in the clear.

'Anyone else?' asked Emily.

'Cliff,' said Ben. 'He smelt of petrol, didn't he?'

'It couldn't *possibly* be him,' insisted Alex. 'I mean—' His voice died away. 'Why would he do it?'

'Yes,' said Emily. 'Surely Cliff couldn't be involved?'

'Money counts for a lot with people.' Ben looked uneasy. 'Bill Buxton could be paying him to do the damage—'

'Just as easily as Jud or Jenny. If Buxton *is* behind all this he could certainly do with an insider,' agreed Kate.

'Could he be using all three of them?' suggested Emily rather wildly.

'The more people involved the greater the risk.' Ben was completely against the idea.

'Suppose Cliff pretended that he believed in Jud to give him a false sense of security?' he added thoughtfully.

'Like he was setting a trap for him?' Emily looked horrified.

'The alternative could be that Cliff really *does* trust Jud and Jud's playing on that, relying on his goodwill to protect him,' said Alex. 'Look – I've known Cliff for years. He'd never get involved in anything like this.'

'There's another alternative, isn't there?' wondered Emily reluctantly. 'Suppose Jud's blackmailing Cliff, forcing him to do a protection job on him.'

'That's certainly another possibility,' Ben replied.

'What about Jenny Rowe? Why's she so suddenly in the clear?' Alex was anxious she shouldn't be allowed to escape.

'She's not,' said Kate. 'She could still be working with Jud somehow.'

'Mrs Petrie's her alibi—' began Emily.

'Is she?' demanded Ben. 'We've only got Jenny Rowe's word for that.'

'So shouldn't we see what Mrs Petrie has to say?'

They all three looked at Kate blankly. 'How?' asked Alex eventually.

'Suppose Ben and I visit the Tudor Café on behalf of Tremaron High's domestic science department.'

There was a stunned silence.

'Because we want some old English recipes,' Kate improvised. 'I'm sure they've got them at the Tudor Café.'

'Your mum will go crazy if she finds out what you're doing,' said Alex.

'That's why she mustn't find out.'

Kate was writing furiously in her case book. 'Let's just recap:

JUD TANNER	Could be blackmailing Cliff or just relying on his trust so he can sabotage the fair for Bill Buxton.
JENNY ROWE	Could be in league with Jud and also working for Buxton. Too much money in her handbag for comfort.
CLIFF BAKER	Is *he* setting up Jud? If so, that cuts out Jenny Rowe.
BILL BUXTON	Behind it all. The paymaster.

Have I left anybody out?' she asked.

The others didn't think so, but Alex again rushed to Cliff's defence. 'He's just not a suspect. I know him too well.'

'That's what Sam Shepherd said about Jenny

Rowe,' pointed out Ben. 'But he doesn't know her at all.'

Alex looked sullen.

Kate checked her watch. 'It's six. Won't the Tudor Café be closed—'

Alex shook his head. 'I know the opening times by heart since we stood outside for so long. Mrs Petrie serves light meals till seven, and I bet they're awful. Runny eggs on burnt toast.'

'Be careful,' warned Emily. 'It would be a pity if your parents decided to drop in for high tea.'

Ben opened the door of the Tudor Café which gave a genteel chime as they entered. The room had Tudor beams, a large hearth with a roaring fire, inglenook seats and a good deal of dark panelling. There was a scattering of chairs and tables, but only one couple in the café, silently eating baked ham and tomatoes.

A young woman in a slightly stained apron approached them, a plastic smile on her lips. 'Table for two?'

'Actually,' said Kate, 'we came to see Mrs Petrie.'

'Do you have an appointment?' The smile curdled on the waitress's lips and she looked disappointed, cheated of even the smallest tip.

'We don't. But it's a school project.' Ben tried to sound casual and confident, but didn't entirely succeed.

'I can ask her but she's very busy you know. I can't say if she'll see you.'

She thumped across the bare oak boards, leaving Kate and Ben to wonder just what Mrs Petrie was doing to make her so busy while the café was empty.

Seconds later, the waitress returned, looking even more put out. 'She'll see you for a few minutes. Follow me.'

Mrs Petrie was somehow much younger than they had expected. She was very plump and wore what seemed to be a large amount of clothes. She had rings on most of her fingers, coils of beads at her throat and her hair was wrapped in a highly coloured scarf. As a result, she exuded a faintly exotic air, as if she was a fortune teller or some kind of mystic.

The stuffy room was crowded with bookcases jammed full of volumes on folklore and ancient wisdom, books that overflowed on to small tables and a big untidy sofa. Mrs Petrie was sitting at a desk, writing in a leather-bound book. She gazed at Kate and Ben over a pair of half-rimmed glasses which were pushed to the end of her nose.

'How can I help?' Her voice was a low purr.

'We're sorry to bother you,' said Kate, 'but we wondered if you could give us any old English recipes for our domestic science class at Tremaron High.'

'Do I look like an old English kind of person?' Mrs Petrie asked sweetly.

'No,' said Kate hastily. 'Of course not. But we know the Tudor Café has a reputation for some brilliant home cooking.'

'It's very sweet of you to say that, my dear,' she purred. 'But I'm afraid the Tudor Café offers a very plain bill of fare. My own interests are elsewhere.' She gazed fondly at her books and papers.

'How do you mean?' blurted out Ben awkwardly.

'I'm only interested in nutritional recipes handed down from medieval sources, I'm afraid. I'm compiling my own book. You mustn't confuse my medieval recipes with home-made English.'

'No,' said Ben with a flash of inspiration, 'we're not. It's just that we have to present a new project for a domestic science prize and what you've just said sounds very interesting. You couldn't – couldn't give us a few tips, could you?'

‘Of course I could,’ said Mrs Petrie in pleased surprise. ‘I must say I *am* getting popular. Perhaps people will buy my book after all.’

‘Popular?’ asked Kate guardedly.

‘Yes. A young lady was in here only this morning, asking about the very same recipes. Spent quite a bit of time with me in fact.’

‘How long?’ asked Ben sharply, without thinking.

‘I beg your pardon?’

‘I mean – how long can you spare people?’ he said quickly. ‘We know how busy you are.’

‘I’m always available to those interested.’ Mrs Petrie was looking gratified.

Kate stepped in quickly in case Ben asked for an exact description of her visitor. ‘Maybe you could just give us a couple of recipes – as a sample.’ She was already feeling a pang of disappointment and was sure that Ben was feeling much the same. If Jenny had been interviewing Mrs Petrie she certainly wouldn’t have had time to reach the fairground and set the Hall of Mirrors on fire.

‘I can do better than that,’ said Mrs Petrie triumphantly. ‘You can try one of them. You may find it a little – different. Then I’ll give you the ingredients.’

‘What’s it called?’ asked Ben warily.

'Frog-spawn jelly – wonderful for fatigue – makes you full of beans.' She rose majestically to her feet and went to a cupboard. 'It's a bit runny, but you *will* have some, won't you?'

'I can't,' said Kate, thinking fast. 'I've got an upset stomach.'

'Oh dear,' said Mrs Petrie in disappointment. 'It's really quite delicious. Will you try some, young man?'

'Er—'

'You really *must*.'

'OK,' said Ben reluctantly. He knew he couldn't present her with the same excuse and he couldn't think of another.

With a pleased smile Mrs Petrie handed him a small plastic bowl of green jelly that seemed to move and heave of its own accord. She placed a plastic spoon in the bowl which was gradually sinking into the slime.

Ben was very pale as he took the bowl, looking down at it with considerable anxiety.

Kate tried to pretend that what was going to happen next wasn't going to happen at all. 'That does look delicious,' she told the beaming Mrs Petrie. 'Can you let us have the recipe?'

'Of course I will, my dear,' she replied. 'First you visit a local pond—'

With a strangled cry, Ben just managed to

balance the bowl on a pile of books before running from the room.

'If you ask me,' said Mrs Petrie sweetly, 'you've *both* got stomach upsets.'

· 11 ·

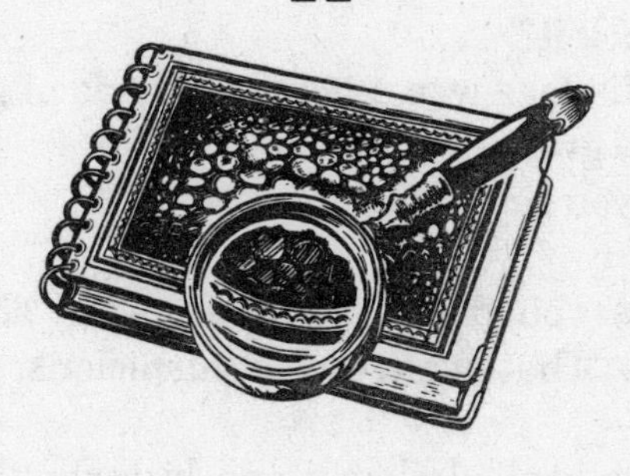

'He came running in searching for the toilet,' said the sour young waitress when Kate emerged from Mrs Petrie's room after an affectionate farewell, the details of the recipe in her pocket. 'And what's more, he's still in there.'

'I'll wait outside. I'm sure my brother won't be long.'

'I hope so. The toilet is for customers' use only.'

Kate glanced round the empty café. There

weren't any customers.

'We're not closed yet,' said the waitress defensively.

Kate opened and closed the chiming door and stood outside on the street where Ben eventually joined her.

'You OK?' she asked.

'Do I look it?'

'No.' His face was a horrible shade of green – almost as green as the jelly.

'Were you sick?' she asked.

'Very.'

'I hope you didn't make a mess,' she said severely. 'That waitress is suspicious enough already—'

'No,' he replied slowly and bitterly. 'I didn't make a mess. But you could say this investigation has turned out to be a bit of a waste of time. If Mrs Petrie's to be believed, Jenny Rowe didn't set one foot outside the Tudor Café.'

'I think Mrs Petrie *is* to be believed,' said Kate, setting off at a brisk pace.

'Walk slowly,' pleaded Ben. 'I can't keep up.'

'As long as you don't *throw* up,' replied his sister unsympathetically.

*

'It's not funny,' said Ben as Alex and Emily laughed uncontrollably over what had happened at the Tudor Café. He was still feeling rather delicate and only Kate was keeping tactfully quiet, despite the fact that Ben was sure her lips were twitching.

They were sitting round the table in the *Spindrift* a little later that evening. It was dark now but the sea was calm and smooth, making little washing noises at the shore.

'I'm not crossing Jenny Rowe off as a suspect,' said Kate firmly. 'We still need to keep an eye on her.'

'But Jud isn't one either.' Alex was disappointed. 'Not for the fire anyway.'

'Which leaves Cliff,' said Emily.

'I just can't believe it's him.' Kate was really convinced. 'He's such a decent person.'

'You're right there,' muttered Alex.

'You don't know him, Kate,' said Ben shortly. 'How can you say that?'

She wasn't in the least put out. 'I've just got a hunch, that's all. No evidence. Not a shred.'

'It seems to me that you and Alex think Cliff can't do any wrong,' said Emily belligerently.

'I can see beyond friendship – believe it or not.' Alex was angry.

'The saboteur could be any of the stall

holders,' said Ben quickly, trying to calm them all down, 'or one of those thugs who were attacking Jud. We'll have to work a rota and keep the fairground under even closer surveillance. Let's say – four hours on and then someone else takes over.'

'That could go on for days,' said Alex.

'It probably will,' pointed out Kate. 'Things may quieten down for a bit, while the police and the fire brigade are around investigating the fire.'

'What's the time?' asked Alex suddenly.

'Half-past seven.'

'Why don't we cycle over to Bill Buxton's Pleasure Park? It would only take us half an hour and maybe we could do some sussing out while we're there,' he added vaguely.

'That's a good idea,' said Kate. 'At least it'll be something to do. But we *must* be back by nine. Mum's on the warpath in case anyone *didn't* notice.'

Collecting their bikes cost them a vital ten minutes, but soon all four were speeding along as fast as they could, trying to keep up with Alex who was in the lead and pedalling hard.

At the rear, Ben, still recovering from the frog-spawn jelly, was concentrating on trying to keep up, whilst Alex was certain that he had suggested a wild goose chase. But to do nothing, to wait for another sabotage attempt, was much worse. What was more, they all knew that a certain amount of resentment had built up between them. Emily, for instance, felt slightly ashamed of herself for attacking Kate and Alex over their support for Cliff. On a broader stretch of road, she cycled alongside Kate and apologized.

'I'm sorry. I just feel a bit left out that's all. Alex seems so close to you both. Sometimes I feel I haven't got anything to contribute.'

'Of course you have,' said Kate. 'You were great in that Shadow Caves mystery. We need you, Emily. You've got to believe me.' Emily smiled at her gratefully.

'Anyway, Alex and I *could* be wrong about Cliff. It is possible.'

Bill Buxton's Pleasure Park was very different from Sam Shepherd's Fairground. Situated in the centre of Penlyn, the place was a mass of flashing lights as dozens of different rides roared and zoomed, hung upside down or roller-coasted at high speed. There were dodgems and giant wheels, caterpillars and switchbacks. There was also a ghost train, a crazy house and dozens of sideshows.

'What now?' asked Ben, as they paused by the gates. 'We can't get in without paying a fortune – and we haven't got any money left, have we?'

Disconsolately, they cycled around the perimeter fence of the pleasure park until they came to a small entrance labelled GOODS ONLY.

'Let's try here,' suggested Alex.

'If we're caught, Buxton will have us for trespassing,' warned Ben. 'We're in enough trouble already.'

Alex glanced behind him for a second and then headed for an old caravan that was parked at the front of the goods entrance.

'Move,' he hissed.

Somehow they all managed to get out of sight as a car noisily turned off the road and a rather battered VW rattled through the gates. Behind the wheel was Jud Tanner.

· 12 ·

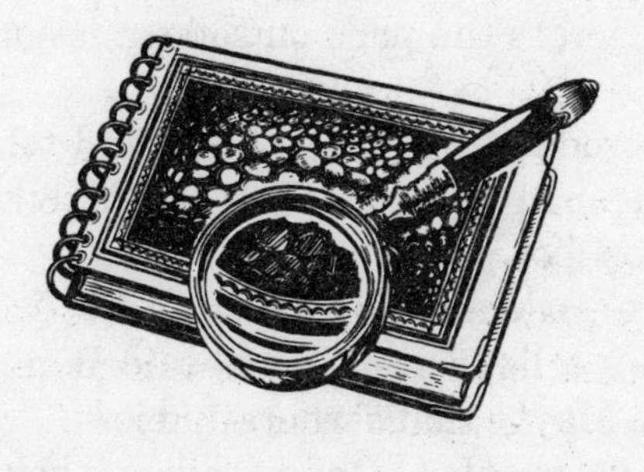

'He could have seen us setting out and followed,' said Emily doubtfully. 'Or maybe he guessed where we were going and came by a different route.'

'What are we going to do?' Ben wondered. They were all at a loss.

'Let's see where he goes,' suggested Kate.

They cycled on down the service road until they reached a dead end, but there was no sign of the VW.

'We must have missed it,' said Ben.

'I'll go back and check.' Emily turned and cycled past a little wood that was littered with old crates and rusting machinery. Amongst the debris was the VW.

Where was Jud? she wondered. Was he somewhere in the wood, or was he already on his way across the park on some mission of his own?

Emily rode back to the others and told them what she had seen. 'Let's hide our bikes and explore on foot.'

'Where?' asked Alex.

'There's a light over there,' said Ben. 'It just came on. Maybe that's where Jud is.'

They concealed their bikes behind a tumbledown shed, and cautiously approached what appeared to be a small office, built of brick and sheet metal. There was one large window and behind it they could see dim and flickering torchlight.

'Keep down,' whispered Kate. 'Let's see what he's up to.'

They crept towards the ugly little building which was at the back of the Crazy House. Flashing lights occasionally caught the sheet metal, making it wink and gleam.

Sure enough, Jud was inside, turning over the

contents of a file and then furtively going through some desk drawers. He seemed to take ages examining each document, completely absorbed. Then he extracted a crumpled scrap of paper which he smoothed out and pored over with great attention. Pressing her face to the dirty glass, Kate could just make out the words: WHITELANDS HUMMING GOOGLIE. MESSAGE RECEIVED AND UNDERSTOOD.

Jud took out a pencil and a piece of paper while she signalled to the others to withdraw.

Hiding behind the shed again, they waited until Jud hurried furtively back to his VW, backed the car out of the rubbish-strewn wood and drove away.

Then the four of them mounted their bikes and pedalled off as fast as they could, half expecting Jud to be lying in wait for them. But there was no sign of the VW, and they made it back to the quayside at Tremaron by just before twenty to nine without further incident.

The harbour wall was deserted and they were able to talk openly in the very brief amount of time they had left.

Kate had already told them what she had seen Jud staring at in the little office, but no one had yet been able to work out what the puzzle meant.

'WHITELANDS HUMMING GOOGLIE,' Kate repeated slowly. 'We've got ten minutes to solve this.'

'It's obviously a code,' said Ben.

'WHITELANDS HUMMING GOOGLIE,' muttered Alex. 'Did Jud understand what it meant?'

'I don't know,' said Kate. 'He could have done. I wonder if it's a warning? Or some kind of instruction?'

'Wait a minute,' said Ben in sudden triumph. 'Take the first three letters – W H G. What could they stand for?'

'They don't join together to make a word,' said Emily. 'And neither do the last three.'

'They might be the *starting* letters of three *different* words.' Ben was now wildly excited. 'Like White Knuckle.'

'Hall of Mirrors,' said Emily quickly.

'And what else?' asked Kate uncertainly.

'They were targets,' said Alex. He was thinking quickly. Then he breathed, 'Ghost Maze.'

'Jud's next target?' asked Emily.

'*Someone*'s next target. We don't know for sure it's Jud,' protested Kate.

'We should go to Uncle Sam,' said Alex. 'Warn him.'

'No.' Kate held back. 'We can't do that. There's still an outside chance he might be involved.'

'Whoever's doing this,' said Ben, 'is trying to make out how dangerous Sam's fairground is. Any insurance claim would drag on for ever so there's not much mileage in that. In the meantime the town council will probably close the place because of lousy safety standards.'

Gloomily Alex began to repeat the damage list. 'The White Knuckle. The council could prove a faulty computer.'

'The Hall of Mirrors,' continued Emily. 'Suppose the fire brigade comes up with an electrical fault – or even just skimping on fire regulations?'

'The Ghost Maze,' said Ben slowly. 'That could be made to look dangerous too. Particularly if punters were riding on it at the time.'

'They're riding on it now,' snapped Kate. Then she remembered. 'No they're not. The place must still be closed because of the fire.' They all gazed back towards the fairground and saw with relief that it was dark.

'We'll have to check out that maze,' said Emily. 'But how are we going to do that if we haven't got any money left?'

'I'll have to raid my savings.' Alex sounded martyred.

'We'll only need to ride the maze once or twice,' said Kate. 'The rest of the time we'll be watching—'

'And spending more money or we'll look suspicious.'

'We'll pay you back,' promised Ben.

'It's not only Uncle Sam who might go bankrupt,' said Alex, looking depressed.

· 13 ·

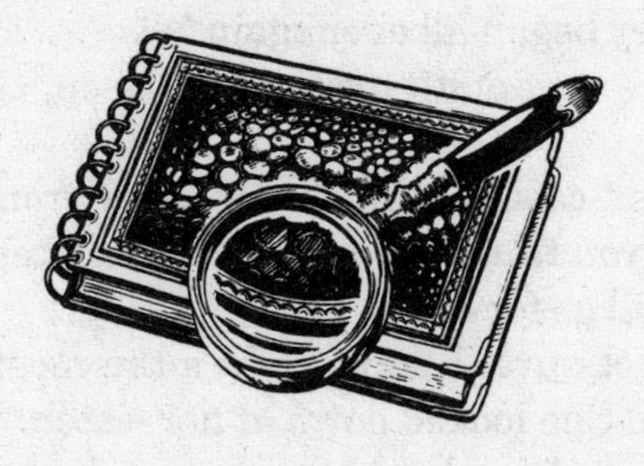

That night Ben dreamt of eating frog-spawn jelly on the Ghost Maze ride. He was sitting next to Mrs Petrie who kept spooning it into his mouth so fast that he was drowning in the stuff. Eventually he shouted, 'No!' so loudly that Kate heard and hurried into his room.

She perched on the edge of the bed, gazing down at his tousled hair and pale, sweating face.

'Jelly?' she asked.

He gulped and looked away. 'Don't talk about it,' he pleaded, 'or I'll be sick again.'

'I've been dreaming too.'

'What about?'

'Sheep jumping over a fence – except they had human faces. The first was Jud, the next was Cliff, the next was Sam, the next was Jenny and then they began all over again.'

'You're meant to drop *off* to sleep, counting sheep.'

'In this case I couldn't get away from them. Who do *you* think is doing all this sabotage?'

'I'd still go for Jud.'

'I'm not sure. I suppose he's the most likely, isn't he?' She looked down at her watch. 'It's just after four. We should get some sleep. Proper sleep. Are you going to be OK? Or will you dream about jelly again?'

Ben burrowed his head under the duvet. 'I won't if you stop going on about it.'

The morning dawned cloudy with a light drizzle, and by eleven the children were in position, stepping up surveillance in the fairground. Alex played a pin-ball machine near his uncle's caravan, having checked that Sam Shepherd was inside, writing up figures in a ledger. Earlier, he had told his nephew the fire brigade suspected arson, but the police were still at an early stage of their investigations. They had questioned most people in the fairground but had not got any clues as to who was responsible.

The fair was open again, but punters were thin on the ground and the emptiness was depressing to everyone.

Emily had the more difficult task of watching Jenny Rowe, whose cash kiosk was near the entrance, just to the right of the rifle range. She had had to pay for session after session, eventually winning a small pink pig which ironically turned out to be a money box.

'Taking a break, are you, love?' asked the eager stall holder. 'Only five goes to get that pig, wasn't it? How about trying for the big fluffy dog then?'

Emily give him a bright smile. 'Do you think I stand a chance?' she asked.

'I should say so.' As far as the stall holder was concerned, Emily was fast becoming a nice little earner.

Jud was moving around the fairground, doing odd jobs at a brisk rate, and Kate had a tough time trying to follow him without looking suspicious. She darted from game to game, rolling a ball here and a coin there, but she got so distracted in the process that one of the stall holders, watching in amazement as she shoved coins into a chute while looking in the opposite direction, commented mildly, 'If you don't concentrate you don't stand a chance.'

'Sorry.' Was that Jud moving behind him? Where was he going now? Why didn't he settle down to one job at a time? He seemed to be everywhere at once.

'There you go again. You like this at school?'

Ben had an easier time with Cliff, who was in the control room of the White Knuckle, intent on ensuring the safety of the few punters as the roller coaster careered over its steel switchback.

Ben had managed to position himself at a What the Butler Saw machine, where he guardedly watched an overweight lady repeatedly kissing an overweight gentleman on a sofa.

Suddenly, Kate was at his side, looking frantic. 'Jud's gone into the Ghost Maze with a spanner. Where are the others? Why didn't we work out some kind of signal?'

'OK. You find Alex and I'll get Emily. Meet at the maze as soon as you can.'

They both sped off in different directions, no longer caring how suspicious they might look, careering around the almost empty fairground.

*

At last Kate found Alex and dragged him towards the Ghost Maze, only to find Ben running towards them with Emily, both out of breath, both looking anxious.

'OK. OK,' said the young girl on the turnstile. 'No need to panic. Plenty of time left for the ghostly ride of a lifetime.'

They piled in, noticing that out of a train of six cars only two were occupied, with a couple of young boys and a middle-aged pair, who were rather self-consciously getting themselves comfortable.

'Try and work out how the maze is laid out,' whispered Ben. 'I've got this feeling we might need a sense of direction.'

The cars clanked and jerked forward, beginning to move slowly towards a set of battered black, rubber doors.

Once inside, chilling screams and eerie laughter echoed about them as a flashing sign said WELCOME TO THE GHOST MAZE. REMEMBER THERE'S NO WAY OUT.

Speeding up, the train headed for the sign and then, with a jerk, veered away, plunging between high, bright green borders made of grinning skulls. Hurtling round the corners, they met animated corpses, skeletons, ghouls and an occasional vampire at every turn. Sometimes the train thundered towards an open coffin, the doors of a vault, a salivating werewolf, and a man whose laughing head turned around on its axis.

The skulls flanked them until the train slowed down at the centre of the maze. Open graves yawned, and instead of names on the tombstones the legends ran: THIS IS FOR YOU – AND YOU – AND YOU – AND ESPECIALLY FOR YOU. UNLESS YOU CAN GET OUT WHICH YOU CAN'T! There was peal upon peal of manic laughter and then another message flashed up: YOU'RE TRAPPED!

The train picked up speed again.

As they rocked round another couple of twists of the maze a banshee leapt out on wire, a headless woman waved and soft cobwebs touched their foreheads. But although the other occupants of the train screamed and screamed again, Alex and Emily, Kate and Ben tried desperately to concentrate on keeping their sense of direction – a virtual impossibility in the whirling darkness. There was no hope of seeing Jud – or anyone else for that matter.

Then, as the train took a sharp left turn, Alex yelled, 'I think we're going back. That ghoul seems familiar. And the vampire—'

Suddenly, without any warning, the train stopped.

At first, the punters imagined the silence to be all part of the ride. Then, after a minute or so of giggling suspense, they began to realize that something had gone horribly wrong and the darkness seemed to press in like a tight black shroud.

'What's going on?' asked one of the boys.

'Have we got to walk back?' asked his companion.

Another lengthy silence followed.

'Isn't there an alarm?' came a woman's voice, shrill and on the verge of hysteria. 'Surely something's wrong.'

'You're not to panic, Mary,' said her husband, his voice shaking. 'I'm sure one of the engineers will be along shortly.'

'I'm not panicking, Peter. I just want to get out.'

'I'm sure one of the engineers will be along shortly.'

'It's very claustrophobic in here—'

'I'm sure one of the engineers will be—'

'If you say that again I'll scream.'

The silence deepened, as if it was a great lake,

swallowing them all up.

At last, Ben said, 'We're going to have to walk.'

No one replied.

'I want to go home,' said one of the young boys abruptly.

'I shall sit here until rescue arrives,' said the woman unsteadily.

'I want to go home,' repeated the boy. 'I want to—'

Suddenly, angry shouting filled the maze, interrupted by a cry of pain and the sound of running footsteps fading away into the distance.

'Who wants to walk back to the entrance?' demanded Alex.

No one replied.

'I think we should all stay where we are,' said the man. 'I'm sure someone will come along any second.'

They all listened to the deep, suffocating silence and heard nothing. Then the woman voiced what was in all their thoughts but which no one had dared to say aloud. 'What was that cry? Is someone injured?' Her voice rose and one of the young boys began to whimper.

'Let's go,' said Ben, trying to sound reassuring. He jumped down to the track and hesitated, wondering which way to go.

'We ought to have brought a torch,' said Alex, irritated by their lack of preparation.

'Our eyes will get used to the dark,' said Emily with sudden confidence. 'Mine are now.'

Slowly, the others jumped down beside Ben, realizing they could just make out dim shapes at least.

'OK,' he said, desperately trying to remember. 'Let's get going. One ghoul to the right, a vampire to the left and a skeleton to the right again.'

'Are you sure?' said Alex doubtfully. 'Wasn't it a vampire to the right, a ghoul to the left and *then* the skeleton to the right again?'

'I thought you two had memorized this,' said Kate crossly, knowing she was being unfair.

'We were *all* memorizing it, weren't we?' accused Alex.

'Yes,' said Emily, trying to back him up. 'But it's like Ben said, a skeleton to the right—'

'I didn't say that,' snapped Ben.

'What *did* you say?' demanded Kate brutally.

'A vampire – I mean a ghoul and—' He paused in confusion as a powerful beam began to move towards them.

· 14 ·

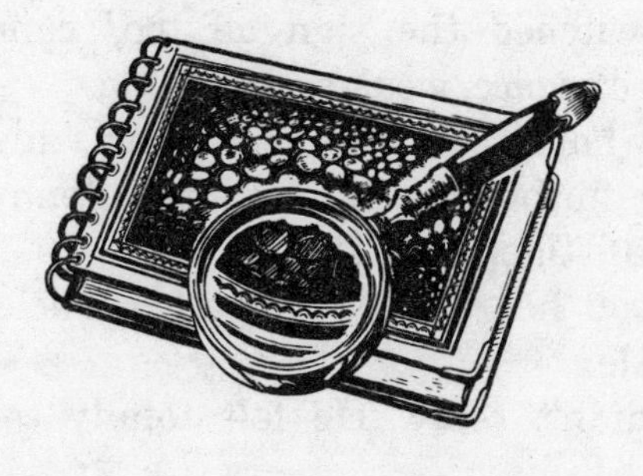

'Who's there?' yelled a familiar voice which they recognized as Jenny Rowe's.

'Us,' yelled Ben. 'Alex and Kate and Emily and Ben. There's been some kind of breakdown. We left the other passengers on the train. A grown-up couple and two young kids.'

'Just stay where you are. We'll come to you.' Did her voice sound warmer or was it just because they so much wanted to be rescued?

They heard a grunt of pain and immediately

the beam pointed downwards.

Who was Jenny Rowe bringing with her, wondered Kate. Who was it who was in so much pain? Was it Jud, or had he hit someone with his spanner? Then they heard her say, 'Come on, Dad. We're still heading towards the emergency exit. They're practically on top of it.'

'He switched the sign off too,' came Sam Shepherd's voice, weak and shaking.

But who is *he*, wondered Ben, his mind working furiously. And why had Jenny Rowe called Sam Shepherd 'Dad'?

'Did you hear what she called Uncle Sam?' hissed Alex.

Ben didn't reply. He felt totally confused, unable to focus.

'I'm certain she said Dad.'

'You must have misheard,' whispered Kate.

'I didn't.'

In the shadow of the flashlight, Jenny Rowe and Sam Shepherd squeezed their way past a plastic vampire.

'What happened?' asked Ben when he saw the blood on Sam's face.

'Trouble,' he replied. 'The attendant called me and said the train hadn't come out and the power had gone off, so like a fool I came straight in. I bumped into someone, didn't I? There's an emergency cut off switch at the top of the track, and he must have got at that. Anyway – he whacked me and did a runner.'

'Didn't you have *any* idea who he was?' demanded Ben.

'He was on the small side I think. Can't be sure, though.'

'Could have been Jud,' said Alex. 'We saw him go in with a spanner.'

'Or Cliff,' put in Ben. 'Jud could have been set up.'

'Or a stranger,' Jenny Rowe pointed out. 'You can't just *assume* it's an inside job.'

'Why did you call Sam Dad?' asked Alex, voicing everyone's thoughts. 'Was that some kind of joke?'

'I don't think the circumstances merited joking,' said Jenny Rowe icily. 'As a matter of fact he *is* my dad.'

'It was a real shock,' said Sam. 'She looked a bit like my wife, but I thought it was just a coincidence.'

Alex stared at him in concern. Had that blow on the head made him imagine things? Jenny didn't look remotely like Aunt Ethel.

'Jenny told me who she was when she rescued me in here. She thought I was dead when she found me. I couldn't take it in – still can't take it in – but I know it has to be true.' Sam turned to Alex. 'I was married before you see. Years ago and it didn't work. Alice went to Devon with our baby Jennifer and I never saw them again. Now my Jenny's back.' His voice broke.

'Why didn't you tell Sam earlier?' demanded Kate.

'I wanted to see for myself what kind of man my father was,' said Jenny slowly. 'Now I know he's one of the good ones. When I came in here to see what had happened and found him hurt – I just had to tell him. It was the right time.' She paused and then said impatiently. 'Well, what are you lot waiting for? I thought you fancied yourselves as detectives.'

'The emergency exit's just here,' said Sam. 'Push the bar and the doors will open. I'll go and rescue the punters.'

The glare of the late morning sun was dazzling as they emerged from the darkness of the Ghost Maze. But as they got used to the light, none of the four of them could believe their eyes. A crowd surrounded the White Knuckle Ride. Unbelievably another crisis was taking place. It's like a war, thought Alex. He felt shell-shocked.

Gazing up, they saw passengers waving

desperately from the roller coaster which they realized, with a thrill of horror, was stuck yet again at the very top. The saboteurs had struck twice this time. Was this to be their final assault on Sam Shepherd's fairground?

'I've had enough of this place,' said one woman to another, dragging away a screaming child. 'It's not safe.'

Kate thought her words exactly summed up what the saboteurs had been trying to achieve and a chill swept through her.

Had they lost the battle? Was his uncle finished? Alex wondered as Kate ran towards the control room of the White Knuckle Ride and flung open the door.

Cliff had Jud by the throat and was pushing him back over the computer, but he rapidly let him go as the four of them stood on the threshold.

Jud collapsed into a chair, gasping for breath.

'I'm sorry,' Cliff mumbled. 'I shouldn't have gone for him. But he proved me wrong. I trusted him, stuck up for him – and then found him reprogramming the computer again. I've been such a fool.'

'He's lying,' gasped Jud. 'He fixed the Ghost Maze and now the White Knuckle. I went into the maze to make a routine check and Cliff must have got in through the emergency doors and waited till I'd finished. I was heading back here when I saw him come out of the maze. But when I asked him what he'd been doing, Cliff went for me.'

Cliff laughed easily, confidently. 'Bill Buxton's been paying you a fortune to wreck our chances, hasn't he? But I haven't got time to argue now. There's people in trouble up there. You kids keep an eye on him, and if he tries to do a runner get Jenny to phone the police.' Cliff grabbed the megaphone and strode outside, addressing those trapped high up on the White Knuckle as calmly as before.

'Please stay where you are,' he shouted. 'I repeat. Please stay where you are. I'm going to wind the ride down manually. There is no danger. Absolutely no danger at all.'

Ben glanced from Cliff to Jud and back again. Who was the saboteur?

They watched Cliff open a small hatch just behind the control room. He bent over some machinery inside and then took out a steel tube which he inserted into a wheel. Suddenly, however, he gazed down in disbelief. 'The cable's been cut – almost half-way through.' He straightened up and shook his fist through the window. 'You did this, Jud, didn't you?'

Alex hurried out of the control room and ran to Cliff's side while the other three remained where they were, all too conscious they were Jud's jailors. But he made no move to escape and remained slumped in the chair, his face expressionless, his eyes glazed.

'You can't wind them down,' said Alex. 'What happens if this cable snaps?'

There was sweat standing out on Cliff's forehead as he gazed up at the roller coaster. 'The ride will start running backwards. I'll have to climb up. There's a manual safety brake that should wedge the cars in position.'

'I'm good at climbing,' said Alex. 'Can't I go with you?'

'No way. You just see Jud doesn't do that runner I reckon he's planning. I'll make sure the punters are safe.'

Cliff pushed past Alex, ran towards the White Knuckle and began to climb the switchback just as Sam Shepherd, Jenny Rowe and the luckless passengers of the Ghost Maze staggered into the sunlight.

'What's Cliff think he's doing?' yelled Sam.

'He's going to put on the emergency brake,' said Alex. 'Someone's stopped the ride and cut some of the cable.'

Sam Shepherd looked so ill that Kate thought

he might collapse at any minute. Then he said, 'That brake's only meant for testing the weight of the ride. If those cars start sliding backwards, then Cliff's going to be in dead trouble.'

Like the punters, thought Alex.

Sam Shepherd stumbled towards the control room and wrenched open the door.

'Just a minute,' he said. 'What's that toolbox doing in here?'

Jud looked up at him sharply. 'What toolbox?'

'That one,' Sam snapped. 'Whose is it?'

'Mine.'

'We followed you,' said Ben quietly while Sam went in and began to rummage through the box, watched intently by Jud. 'Did you see us?'

'Followed me? Where?'

'To Bill Buxton's Pleasure Park last night.'

'I was following *you*.' Jud shrugged, tearing his eyes away from Sam Shepherd's search, forcing himself to focus on Ben. 'I saw you riding off on your bikes and guessed where you were going. I thought you might have gone to suss out Buxton well before then – although what you would have found up there I wouldn't like to say.'

'We went because there was nothing else to do,' admitted Ben. 'It was a lucky strike that you followed us. We might not have found anything – but you did, didn't you?'

'I didn't want you to run into any danger,' continued Jud. 'Buxton's a thug – and he's got plenty more thugs working for him. But when I got there I lost you. Either that or you weren't going where I thought you were going. Anyway, I decided to have a look round so I forced the lock on his office—'

'And went through his papers,' finished Emily. 'We were watching you.'

'I wasn't doing anything wrong. Anyway – I had to do something. I guessed I was going to be stitched up. In the end all I found was this weird message.'

'Buxton was careless not to destroy it,' said Kate. 'Perhaps someone came in and he just stuffed it to the back of the drawer.'

'What did all that gobbledegook mean anyway?' asked Jud.

As she told him they all watched his reaction. He seemed utterly bewildered and his performance – if it was a performance – was convincing.

'I wonder who the message was for,' said Ben. 'We thought you recognized it, had seen those words somewhere before.'

'You can search me,' said Jud quickly, back on the defensive again. 'I never saw any of it before.'

Sam Shepherd was still going through the toolbox. Then, very gingerly, he pulled out a large pair of cutters. 'These belong to you?'

'They're Cliff's,' Jud said, his face white and strained.

'You *would* say that, wouldn't you?' Jenny Rowe commented.

As Alex returned to the control room, Sam Shepherd and Jenny Rowe hurried out, only to see Cliff rapidly climbing towards the stranded passengers of the White Knuckle Ride.

'We've found some cable cutters in this toolbox. Jud says they're Cliff's,' said Kate uneasily. 'I'm going to wrap them up in these rags. Just in case they've got any fingerprints on them.'

'Do you think Cliff would climb all the way up there to try and rescue those people – when he might get killed – do you think he'd do all that if he was guilty?' Alex was very angry.

'Cliff always was ambitious. You say Buxton gave him three targets and now he's claimed a fourth – the White Knuckle Ride again. I call that arrogance – unless there was a last minute instruction,' said Jud bitterly.

'You're not thinking straight, Jud,' said Emily quickly. 'We can't just take your word for it, can we? You've admitted this is your toolbox. Why should we believe the cutters are Cliff's?'

'I don't know how to convince you.' Jud was desperate now.

'Cliff's up there climbing to the rescue,' said Kate. 'He *looks* like a hero. How can you prove he's not?'

'That's just it,' said Jud miserably. 'I can't. By sending a coded message, Buxton's been clever. No phone calls. No meets. Just a confirmation all was understood.'

'Who could have delivered the coded messages?' asked Ben.

'It must be someone who had access to this fairground – but also to the Pleasure Park,' replied Kate. She thought carefully and suddenly her mind reeled as she remembered watching old Sal creaking into the fairground on her new bike, ready to take over her shift on the hoopla stall.

Before anyone could ask her what she was doing, Kate had darted out of the control room and over to Sam Shepherd, who was gazing up at Cliff.

'Did any of your employees ever work for Bill Buxton. Recently I mean?'

All his concentration, however, was on what was happening above him.

‘I can’t think about things like that now,’ said Sam. ‘Not with Cliff up there in danger.’

‘You’ve *got* to,’ said Kate. ‘It’s vitally important.’

He gazed down at her impatiently. ‘There’s only old Sal. She had a row with Buxton and brought her hoopla stall over here. She’s a hard worker and—’

‘When did she come?’

‘Not that long ago. Couple of months or so—’

Kate turned away and ran back into the fairground.

Old Sal on her bike, that familiar figure cycling through all weathers. On her bike. That brand *new* bike. That brand new bike which could have been supplied by her ex-employer with whom she had never really had a row, but instead had been put in as a plant, to act as a courier, to ensure that the sabotage targets were set up.

For a moment, Kate turned back to gaze up at Cliff. He was on the track now, reassuring the passengers while a patter of applause floated up from below. She knew she had to work fast, knew she would have to confront the old woman if they were to prove anything at all. Jud and Cliff were still running neck and neck as suspects, and old Sal, if she *was* the courier, could just as easily be running messages for either of them.

Kate knew she had to get a result before Cliff climbed down from the White Knuckle Ride to his hero's welcome.

She found old Sal at the back of her stall, sitting on a box and drinking coffee with her shining new bike propped up behind her.

'You brought those instructions from Bill Buxton, didn't you?' Kate said brightly, in a matter-of-fact voice, hoping that she could unsettle the old lady with a first strike.

'Eh?'

Patiently, Kate repeated her question.

'You out of your mind?' Was there a flicker of fear in old Sal's eyes?

'It's all up,' Kate persisted. 'We know everything.'

'You *are* out of your mind. Coming up to a respectable woman without a by your leave and accusing—'

'Buxton bought that new bike for you, didn't he?' continued Kate. 'For services rendered.'

'How dare—'

'And everyone knows it.'

The flicker of fear was back.

'It's all over,' said Kate. 'Cliff's confessed. He's

grassed you up. That's why he's trying to make amends – get the customers out of danger. He told Mr Shepherd all about you.'

The old woman's lips were moving but no sound came out. Clearly she was terrified. 'I'm a respectable woman—' Sal began again.

'Of course you are,' said Kate with much less aggression in her voice. 'You probably didn't understand the messages you were taking.'

'I certainly didn't.'

Kate's sudden triumph was difficult to conceal. She'd cornered Sal, but would she be able to pin her down? She was sure the old woman was deeply cunning.

'It wasn't your fault,' said Kate persuasively. 'At least – not really. If you tell me what happened, then the police will go easy on you.'

'Tell *you*!' Sal looked at her with withering scorn. 'Tell a child my private business?' Kate felt a sinking feeling in the pit of her stomach. Was she going to lose after all?

'The police will be on their way soon, and of course they'll want to interview you. But I could tell them you didn't understand. Don't forget that Cliff has spoken to—'

'All right. I didn't do anything.' There was a wheedling note in Sal's voice now. 'You'll put in a good word for me—'

'Only if you tell me exactly what happened.'

'I didn't know what was going on—'

'Tell me,' said Kate sharply. 'We haven't got much time.'

'All right. I brought those notes in my saddle bag.'

'On the bike Buxton bought you.'

'It was a goodbye present.' Sal sniffed.

'Who did you give the notes to?'

'Cliff.'

'Did he reply?'

'He gave me one to take back just repeating the message he'd been sent. And then there was one more.'

'Have you got it now?' demanded Kate, trying to keep the excitement out of her voice.

There was silence.

'Where is it?'

'I can't—'

'Where *is* it?'

Sal shrugged and shuffled over to a steel box at the back of the hoopla stall. Underneath was a neatly folded note.

'Show it to me.'

'You'll speak up for me?' Sal whined.

'I promise.'

'Here you are then.' She handed over the note

which read: WHITELANDS HUMMING GOOGLIE WHITELANDS. AND THAT'S THE END OF IT.

'You know what this means?' asked Kate, gazing at Sal's inscrutable features.

'Never had a clue. Right load of rubbish to me. Mumbo jumbo. Two men playing silly games.'

'All right,' said Kate. 'I just want to show it to Sam.'

'You'll do no such thing!' Sal's eyes narrowed. Did she realize she'd just been tricked?

Sal began to shout and swear as Kate raced back to Sam Shepherd, who was still in the crowd watching Cliff.

'Lend me that megaphone,' she said. 'I've got an important message for Cliff.'

'I can't do that,' said Sam. 'You might scare him.'

'He's got to know,' said Kate. 'It's urgent.'

'What's going on?' Ben, Alex, Emily and Jenny Rowe gazed anxiously at her as Sam Shepherd reluctantly handed over the megaphone.

'Cliff?'

He didn't react immediately, apparently still reassuring the terrified passengers on the White Knuckle Ride.

'Cliff?' Still holding on to the car he gazed

down at her. 'I have a message for you. WHITELANDS HUMMING GOOGLIE WHITELANDS. AND THAT'S THE END OF IT.'

Cliff stared down. He didn't move. It was as if he was never going to move again.

· 15 ·

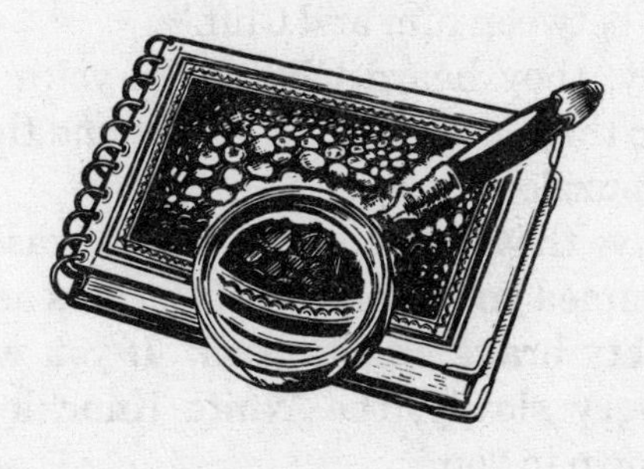

'It's your message to Bill Buxton, isn't it, Cliff?' Kate continued through the megaphone. 'White Knuckle. Hall of Mirrors. Ghost Maze. White Knuckle again.' She paused. 'And it's true – that would be the end of it—'

'What's going on?' yelled Sam Shepherd. He looked bewildered and afraid.

'Don't upset my father,' complained Jenny Rowe. 'He can't take much more.'

'I'm not,' said Kate. 'He ought to be pleased.

The mystery's solved.'

'Where did you get that note?' asked Alex. He was deeply shocked.

'Old Sal. I'm sorry I didn't have time to explain but it all happened so quickly. The connection, I mean. The new bike. The fact she had worked for Buxton. She was the ideal courier between him and Cliff.'

Dimly, they heard Cliff's thin voice floating down to them from a great height and the crowd looked puzzled.

Slowly, they made out what he was saying. 'I've jammed on the brakes of the cars as well as the safety brake on the track. If you wind the cable very slowly, the White Knuckle should coast down to you.'

Sam grabbed the megaphone from Kate. 'Get on the ride, Cliff. We can sort all this out on the ground.'

'No way,' came the distant voice. 'I'm staying up here.'

'Why?'

'I'm staying up here until that girl admits she's telling lies.'

'She can't do that,' yelled Jud, who had just emerged from the control room. 'She's telling the truth and that's all there is to it. Let me come up and talk to you.'

'You come up here – and I'll—' Cliff's voice was very faint and they could only just make out what he was saying.

'This is stupid, Cliff,' bellowed Sam Shepherd through the megaphone. 'Just plain stupid. We can talk this through on the ground. I'm not calling the police.'

'You'll have to eventually,' muttered Jud.

'Come down!'

'No chance.' Cliff was sitting on the top-most loop of the roller coaster. 'No chance at all.'

With a squealing of metal, the White Knuckle slowly descended the gradient as Jud continuously cranked the ride down.

'Where's Alex?' said Ben suddenly.

'There he is.' Emily's voice was sharp with fear. Alex was climbing the framework of the roller coaster as fast as he could.

'They could both be killed,' Jenny gasped.

'Let Alex see what he can do,' Sam muttered. 'That lad's got guts.'

'We can't stand by and do nothing,' Jenny yelled at him. 'Call the fire brigade.'

Sam Shepherd slowly turned back to the kiosk.

Alex climbed purposefully, surprised at the strength of the wind. It wasn't a particularly difficult ascent, but Alex felt light and insubstantial, fear clawing at him now as it had never done before. Suddenly he could hardly breathe, and his arms and legs began to weaken. What was happening to him? He had never been afraid of heights before. It was Ben who—

'Watch it!' Cliff's voice was quiet but full of authority. 'Keep away from me.'

Alex gazed up to see him standing on the track, just a few metres above him.

'You were a fool to come up here. You'd better start climbing down right away.'

'I don't think I can,' said Alex.

'Why not?'

'Somehow on the way up I got scared. I can't move.'

'So you want me to come down with you?'

Alex was silent.

'That's an old trick,' said Cliff mockingly.

'How long are you going to stay up here?'

'Long enough.'

'For what?'

'I don't know.'

Alex's fear increased. Was Cliff going to throw himself off?

'Did you do it?' Despite the obvious danger, he knew he had to ask. 'Did you sabotage the rides?'

There was a long, long silence.

'Yes,' Cliff whispered at last.

'Why?'

'Buxton was blackmailing me.'

'What about?'

'I did something incredibly stupid a couple of months ago. I got persuaded to do a burglary with a pack of yobs. The trouble is the yobs worked for Buxton. They photographed me.'

'It was a set up,' said Alex. 'It must have been.'

'To use me as an insider down here,' agreed Cliff.

'Why did you do the burglary?' asked Alex gently.

'I was broke. I'd been in debt for quite a while. It was a temptation. I don't know how these things happen.' Cliff paused and gazed down at the ground. 'I wonder what falling really feels like. Could it be like flying?'

'No,' said Alex, beginning to feel sick. 'Don't, Cliff. Please don't.'

'I deliberately set up Jud, tried to set him up like Buxton did me. But he's innocent. I was desperate but that's no excuse. I didn't want to hurt anyone either. That kid Rob just walked into the Hall of Mirrors after that stupid sign had fallen down. Not that you'll believe me.'

'What about Sam?' asked Alex.

'I told Buxton that was to be the end of it – that I wouldn't do any more – but Sam can look after himself.'

'You know he can't. Did you realize Jenny was his daughter? Came to find him after years away.'

'How cosy.' There was a sour note in Cliff's voice now and Alex realized he had said completely the wrong thing. The band of nausea and fear heightened inside him. 'I'm a failure, aren't I? If I had the money I'd go to London. Be someone. Now I'm going to be nicked. You can't deny that.'

'Sam might stand up for you.'

'Him? After what I did? Don't forget I was his little wonder boy. He trusted me.'

There was another silence between them while the wind rattled in the track and the ground seemed to reach up to Alex with a great swirling hand. 'I'm going to fall,' he whispered.

'Don't give me that.'

'I can't hang on.'

'Stop the play-acting.'

'Look at me,' yelled Alex. 'Just look. Can't you see?'

Cliff stared down at his pale, sweating face, seeing the glazed terror in his eyes and knew he was telling the truth. 'I'll be with you in a second,' he said abruptly.

When Cliff had clambered down to his level, he placed a strong arm around Alex's waist. 'Don't be afraid. We'll be all right.'

'I suppose you think I tricked you—'

'Just concentrate on the climb.'

Together, they slowly descended the steel superstructure of the roller coaster, and as Cliff and Alex neared the ground the crowd roared in appreciation.

'You'll stay in Tremaron, won't you?' asked Alex. 'I mean after the – the—'

'Stretch?' said Cliff bleakly. 'I could go down for a long time for this.'

'When it's over, you could work on the boats.'

'That's for the fishing families.'

'When my dad hears what you've done for me – you *will* be family.'

'Perhaps,' said Cliff.

Despite everything, Alex was elated as the applauding crowd surrounded them, but the feeling immediately disappeared as the two policemen pushed their way through. In the background he could hear the sirens as the fire brigade approached the fairground for the second time in two days.

'Clifford Andrew Baker—' But Alex didn't

want to hear any more.

He touched Cliff's wrist and whispered, 'We'll be waiting for you. All of us. You belong to Tremaron.'

As Ben, Kate and Emily anxiously checked that Alex was, at least, physically unharmed, Sam Shepherd pushed his way through the crowd, followed by Jenny Rowe.

'I just wanted to thank you lot,' he said. 'I'm determined this fairground's going to survive – *and* win back the punters. As for Buxton, the police will make all the connections.'

'Thank you from me, too.' For the first time there was a smile on Jenny Rowe's face. 'Particularly after all the trouble I got you into with your mum.'

'Jenny will help me recover,' said Sam. 'Jud's going to be appointed senior engineer.' He turned to Alex. 'I'd like to hear what Cliff said. Was there some reason for him doing all this to me?'

Alex nodded. 'There was,' he said.

'Come and talk to me in the caravan,' said Sam, putting his arm round Alex's shoulders.

Slowly they walked away.

'That's another mystery solved,' said Emily. But she was close to tears as she watched Cliff talking to the police.

'At least Sam's found a daughter,' said Kate.

'Yes,' replied Ben slowly, watching Cliff walking towards a police car. 'But solving mysteries isn't just for fun. There's a sad part too.'

'That doesn't mean we're not going to solve another one,' said Kate firmly.

'You bet we are,' replied Emily. 'We're all in this together.'

The Mystery of
Bloodhound Island

Who is the stranger signalling to the island?

Ben, Kate and Alex are sure the new guest at Marlow House has booked in under a false name. They decide to follow him to Bloodhound Island. There, not only are the hounds waiting for them, but the people in the old house have a dark secret.

The Mystery of The Shadow Caves

Who is hiding in the shadow caves?

Ben, Kate and Alex have a new mystery to solve, this time with the help of Emily, whose Uncle Roy has gone missing. Together, they explore the caves, crack the smugglers' code, brave the 'flying mice' and discover the secret at the end of the dark tunnels.

The Mystery of Captain Keene's Treasure

Who will be first to discover the treasure?

Captain Keene comes to stay at Marlow House, searching for his long-lost family fortune. He has half the treasure map but his rival has the other half. Ben, Kate, Alex and Emily, together with their new friend Jamie, want to help Captain Keene, but when the hunt moves to the underground workings of a local tin mine, they are all plunged into danger.